MI

Centenary Collection

**Celebrating 100 years of romance with
the very best of Mills & Boon**

*First published in Great Britain 2008
by Harlequin Mills & Boon Limited,
Eton House, 18-24 Paradise Road, Richmond, Surrey TW9 1SR*

© Susan Napier 1995

ISBN: 978 0 263 86641 4

76-0608

*Harlequin Mills & Boon policy is to use papers that are
natural, renewable and recyclable products and made from
wood grown in sustainable forests. The logging and
manufacturing processes conform to the legal environmental
regulations of the country of origin.*

*Printed and bound in Spain
by Litografia Rosés S.A., Barcelona*

Vendetta

by

Susan Napier

⊚™ MILLS & BOON®
Pure reading pleasure

Susan Napier is a former journalist and scriptwriter who turned to writing romantic fiction after her two sons were born. She lives in Auckland, New Zealand with her journalist husband, who generously provides the ongoing inspiration for her fictional heroes, and two temperamental cats whose curious paws contribute the occasional typographical error when they join her at the keyboard. Born on St Valentine's Day, Susan feels that it was her destiny to write romances and, having written over thirty books for Mills & Boon, still loves the challenges of working within the genre. She likes writing traditional tales with a twist, and believes that to keep romance alive you have to keep the faith – to believe in love. Not just in the romantic kind of love that pervades her books, but in the everyday, caring-and-sharing kind of love that builds enduring relationships. Susan's extended family is scattered over the globe, which is fortunate as she enjoys travelling and seeking out new experiences to fuel her flights of imagination.

Susan loves to hear from readers and can be contacted by e-mail through the website at www.harlequinpresents.com

CHAPTER ONE

THE time had come.

Ten years…

For ten years he had looked forward to this moment with a savage anticipation that had blotted out all lesser ambitions. He had forced himself to watch, to wait, to plan, to carry on with the rest of his life as if revenge had not become the pivot of his existence.

Of course, outside the waiting, the plotting, he had gone through all the right motions, maintaining the fiction of Christian forgiveness…smiling, talking, moving, interacting with those around him, accepting their praise for his achievements, cultivating their admiration and envy, consolidating his wealth. But none of it had had any meaning, any reality for him.

The admiration, the envy, the wealth were necessary only as a source of power. The power to see justice done. The power to punish…

He pressed his right hand on the hard, highly polished surface of his desk, watching the faint mist of heat from his skin bloom across the cool, dark surface between his splayed fingers. A heavy gold ring engraved with an entwined briar and snake on the flat shield flashed in the firelight, the only source of light in the coldly elegant room, as he turned his hand over and stared at the bold tracery of life-lines on his palm. They mocked him with their energy. He had had such grand hopes of life until *she* had come along and casually crushed them.

But now the long, bitter years of waiting were over. He finally had her exactly where he wanted her…in the palm of his powerful hand. And the timing was perfect. She thought that she was safe. She thought that she had got away with it, that everyone had forgotten her crime. Soon, very soon, she would learn differently. There was no statute of limitations on murder.

He curled his fingers inward to form a brutal fist. All he had to do now was close the trap and watch her futile struggles to free herself. She would probably weep and cry innocence, or bluster and threaten, or, better still, cringe and beg for his entertainment. Then he would strip away her pride and her self-respect and stand witness to the death, one by one, of all her hopes and dreams. It was an image that he treasured in the depths of his embittered soul.

He picked up the squat crystal glass next to his hand and took a long swallow of potent, twelve-year-old Scotch. The raw, smoky bite at the back of his throat was pleasurable, but it was no match for the intoxicating taste of revenge that was flooding his senses. For the first time in a decade, he felt almost whole again.

The time had come…

CHAPTER TWO

VIVIAN took the last two steps in one grateful stride and then paused for breath, forcing herself to look back down the narrow staircase that was chipped out of the rocky face of the cliff.

In spite of the fact it was a cold and blustery day, typical of New Zealand's autumn, sweat was trickling down her torso inside her cream blouse and her palm had felt appallingly slippery on the single, stout wooden rail that had been the only barrier between her and the rock-strewn, sea-green oblivion below.

She shuddered faintly as she watched the two men far below, unloading the cargo from the hold of the squat little ferry-boat.

Reaction hit and Vivian swallowed, her dry mouth suddenly thick with moisture. Her legs felt like jelly and she swayed, fighting the urge to sink weakly to the ground.

She pressed a hand to her abdomen, trying to control the unpleasant churning feeling as she turned away and followed the sharply rising, stony path up through the low, scrubby trees. She had to get a grip on herself before she reached her destination. She smoothed down her neat dark green skirt and adjusted the matching blazer as she went, nervously switching the soft-sided leather satchel from one sweaty hand to the other as she tried to calm herself by projecting a mental aura of professionalism.

She had a reputation to uphold. She was here as a representative of Marvel-Mitchell Realties to close a vital property deal. A lot was depending on her. It wasn't just the money, but the future happiness of people that she loved that was at stake.

It hadn't helped that what she had been told was a forty-minute journey from the north-east coast of the Coromandel Peninsula to the island had actually taken over an hour and a half in very choppy seas. After a rushed three-hour drive from Auckland last evening, and an anxious, wakeful night in an uncomfortable motel bed, her close encounter with the Pacific Ocean had not been pleasant.

Since her destination was the private island of a millionaire, Vivian had naïvely expected a luxury launch or hydrofoil to be her mode of transport, not the ugly old tub that she had been directed to at Port Charles. She had also expected the island to be a lush private sanctuary, with beautiful white-sand beaches and flourishing vegetation, rather than a wind-swept, surf-lashed rock in the middle of nowhere. Although the name should have given her a clue, she thought wryly.

Nowhere. She had thought it quaint; now she realised it had been highly descriptive!

What kind of man would drag someone out all this way to conclude a business deal that would have been better, and more safely handled in a city office? Unfortunately, she thought she knew exactly: a man bent on causing trouble. A machiavellian man who would not be appeased by an easy victory. If she was to thwart any of his aims she would have to play his game first.

Vivian came through a small, wind-mutilated grove of low-growing trees and halted, her mouth falling open in shock.

Across a small ridge, perched on a flat tongue of land at the end of a rocky promontory, was a lighthouse. If she hadn't been so busy hanging miserably over the rail of the boat, wondering whether to cast up her rushed motel breakfast into the sea, she would have seen the tall white tower as they approached the island.

She lifted bleak eyes from the wide concrete base, up, up past the vertical line of four tiny windows to stare at the open balcony just below the diamond-shaped glass panes that housed the light. How many stairs to get to the top of *that?*

Her appalled gaze sank back down again and settled with overpowering relief on the low, white-painted concrete building that adjoined the towering structure. A keeper's cottage.

She got a grip on herself. No need to let your imagination run wild, Vivian. All New Zealand lighthouses were now automated. It might even have been decommissioned. She had no business with lighthouses. It was the man in the nice, ordinary, *low* building beside it that she had come to see!

The narrow pathway across the short ridge was fenced on both sides with white pickets, offering her at least a notion of security as the wind swept up one side of the steep, rocky face and wrenched at her hair and clothes with berserk glee. She touched each picket with her free hand as she passed, counting to take her mind off what lay at either side, aware that her neat bun was unravelling more with every step.

By the time she reached the stout, weathered timber door, she was resigned to looking like a freak. A quick glance at her reflection in the curtained window beside the door confirmed the worst. Her shoulder-length hair, inclined to be wild and woolly at the best of times, was making the most of its partial freedom in the moisture-laden air, and there was no time to try and torture the tight ginger curls back into businesslike obedience. Hurriedly Vivian pulled out the few remaining pins. Now, instead of resembling a lop-sided hedgehog, she merely looked like a frightened lion.

She took a deep breath, straightened the side-seams of her skirt, and knocked loudly.

After several moments she knocked again, then again. Finally she tried the door-handle and found to her surprise that it opened easily. She tentatively edged across the threshold.

'Hello, is anybody there? Mr Rose? Mr Rose!' The door closed behind her with a weighty clunk, sounding unpleasantly like the door to a cell.

She walked warily down the short narrow hall and into a large room, sparsely furnished in everything except books—walls of them.

A long, well-used, brown leather couch was drawn up in front of a coal-blackened fireplace and there was a big roll-top desk and chair beside a window overlooking the sea. Another small port-hole window among the books showed the smooth white rise of the adjoining lighthouse tower. There were a few rugs on the polished hardwood floor and a large, smooth-sided antique chest that obviously doubled as a coffee-table, but there were no ornaments or plants, paintings or photographs. Nothing that betrayed the excessive wealth of the owner. Nothing but the books to give the room character…and a rather daunting one at that, thought Vivian, eyeing some of the esoteric titles.

Like the adjacent lighthouse, the house was obviously designed to withstand the constant buffeting of seastorms, the interior walls made of the same thick, rough-cast cement as the outer shell. She wondered nervously whether perhaps it was also designed to endure buffetings from within. The mysterious and formerly benignly eccentric Mr Rose, with whom Marvel-Mitchell Realties had dealt quietly and successfully for years via lawyer, letter and fax, was shaping up to be a chillingly ruthless manipulator. She didn't doubt for one minute that this wait was designed to make her sweat.

Unless he had never intended to turn up at all.

Vivian shivered. She put her briefcase down by the desk and began to pace, trying to burn off her increasing tension. There were no clocks in the room and she checked her watch frequently as ten minutes ticked slowly past. The captain had said the boat would be leaving again in an hour. If Mr Rose hadn't arrived by then she would simply leave.

To pass the time, she re-applied her lipstick and brushed her hair, cursing herself for not tucking extra hairpins into her bag, when suddenly her restless thoughts were drowned out by a loud, rhythmic beating that seemed to vibrate through the walls. Vivian turned towards the window to see a sleek white helicopter descending towards a flat circle of tussock just below the cottage.

She felt her temper fizzle bracingly as the craft settled to rest and the door opened and two men got out, heads ducked low as they battled the whirlwind created by the slowing blades.

Nicholas Rose had a helicopter! Instead of her spending an eternity on a heaving boat, he could have had her *flown* out to the island in minutes! For that matter, he could probably have got to Auckland and back in the time it had taken her to cross the angry patch of water.

She watched as the first passenger, a huge, blond bear of a man in jeans and a sheepskin jacket, stood back and respectfully allowed the man in the dark blue suit to pass him.

Vivian studied the man whom she had travelled all this way to see. Even bowed over, he was tall, and he looked lean and fit, with dark hair and a face that, as he glanced up towards the house, was hard and rugged. He grinned at something that was said behind him and her heart leapt with hope as the grimness dropped away from him and he looked comfortingly sane and civilised. The other one, the beefy blond who shadowed his footsteps with a cat-like alertness, had bodyguard written all over him. They disappeared around the back of the cottage. Vivian was facing the door, her hands clasped nervously behind her, when finally, after another agonised age, it opened.

She bit off a frustrated groan when the jeans-clad figure stepped into the room. Another carefully orchestrated delay, no doubt designed to undermine further her dwindling confidence. Or was the bodyguard here to check her for concealed weapons?

Her eyes darted to his face and the breath caught with a shock in her throat. There was a black patch over his left eye, a thin scar running vertically from his hairline to the top of the concealing inverted triangle and from beneath it down over his high cheekbone to the slanting plane of his cheek. The other eye was light brown, and Vivian's gaze hastily skidded down, afraid he would think she was staring.

His mouth was thin and his face uncompromisingly square and deeply tanned, his thick, straight hair—wheat-gold at the ends and several shades darker at the roots—raked carelessly back from the scarred forehead by fingers and the wind, the shaggy ends brushing the upturned collar of his jacket. Darker gold glinted on the angles of the jutting jaw as his head shifted, revealing at least a day's growth of beard. Even with the eye-patch and the scar he was good-looking, in a reckless, lived-in, don't-give-a-damn kind of way.

Without speaking, he shouldered out of the hip-length jacket and she could see that its bulk had given her a deceptive impression of the man. He wasn't really the behemoth he had first appeared. Although his wine-red roll-necked sweater moulded a fairly impressive pair of shoulders, and was stretched to accommodate a deep chest, his body narrowed to a lean waist and hips that indicated not an ounce of unnecessary fat. His legs were very long, the muscles of his thighs thick enough to strain the faded denim. His hands, as he tossed the discarded jacket effortlessly halfway across the room to land over the back of the couch, were strong and weathered. Big, capable hands. Capable of hurting…or healing, she thought, startled at the unlikely notion that came floating up through her sluggish brain.

He leaned back against the door, snicking it closed

with a shift of his weight, bending his knee to brace the sole of a scuffed leather boot on the wood behind him, crossing his arms over his chest. Vivian forced her gaze to rise again, to discover that she wasn't the only person who appeared to be shocked into a momentary trance. The single, brown eye was unblinkingly studying her, seemingly transfixed by the vivid aureole of hair surrounding her tense face.

Another man with conventional ideas about feminine beauty! She knew her own myriad imperfections well enough; she didn't need his startled stare to remind her. As if the scalding brightness of her hair wasn't enough, her green eyes had the garish brilliance of cheap glass, hardly muted by the lenses of her round spectacles, and a mass of ginger freckles almost blotted out her creamy skin.

Vivian's left hand lifted to smooth down the springy ginger mane around her shoulders, and she smiled tentatively at him, flushing when he didn't respond. A small freckled pleat appeared just above the gold wire bridge of her glasses, and she adjusted them unnecessarily on her straight nose, giving him the 'tough' look that she had practised in the motel mirror the previous night.

'Well, well, well…the Marvel-lous Miss Mitchell, I presume?'

His voice was like silk drawn over rough gravel, sarcastically smooth with a rustling hint of hard, underlying crunch.

A voice used to giving orders. To being obeyed. No polite deference or preening arrogance here. Just utter authority.

Vivian clenched her hands behind her back as the unpalatable truth burst upon her.

She would have far preferred to deal with the civilised Suit! A Suit might be persuaded to sacrifice a small victory for an immediate, larger gain.

This man looked too unconventional, too raw-edged, too primitive ever to have heard of the words 'negotiated surrender'. He looked like a man who enjoyed a fight—and had had plenty of them.

Looking defeat in the face, Vivian knew there was no going back. She *had* to try and beat him at his own game. But no one said she had to play it solely by his rules.

CHAPTER THREE

'THE elusive Mr Rose, I presume?' Vivian echoed his mocking drawl, hoping that she sounded a lot more in control of herself than she felt.

There was a small, challenging silence. He inclined his head, still studying her with the arrested fascination of a scientist confronting a new form of life.

Vivian smoothed her hands nervously down the side-seams of her skirt, and to her horror her fingers encountered the crumpled tail of her blouse trailing from beneath the back of her unbuttoned jacket. Somehow it must have worked free on that nerve-racking climb. Trying to maintain her dignity, she continued to meet his dissecting stare coolly, while surreptitiously tucking her blouse back into the waistband of her skirt.

He noticed, of course, and a curious flicker lightened his expression before it settled back into brooding aggression.

'So…do we now blithely proceed from our mutual presumptions, or do we observe strict propriety and introduce ourselves properly?'

His murmur was rife with hidden meanings, and Vivian

hesitated, wondering whether she was reading her own guilt into his words.

'Uh—well, I think we know who we are…' She closed her eyes briefly, cursing herself for her faltering of courage at the critical moment.

When she opened them again, he was metaphorically crouched in waiting.

'I think, therefore I am?' he said softly. 'Very profound, my dear, but I'm sure Descartes intended his philosophy to be applied to something more meaningful than social introductions. However, far be it from me to contradict a lady, particularly such a highly qualified one as yourself. So, we have an agreement that I'm Nicholas Rose of Nowhere and you are Miss Mitchell of Marvel-Mitchell Realties. Welcome to my world, Miss Mitchell.'

He kicked himself away from the door and walked swiftly towards her, hand outstretched. Without looking down, she was aware that he limped. She was also aware of the savage pride in the single, glittering eye which effortlessly dominated her attention. It seemed to flame with a strange inner light, until the almond-brown iris was shot with blazing spears of gold as he came to a stop in front of her, closer than was comfortable or courteous, towering over her by at least six inches as he insolently invaded her personal space.

She accepted his proffered hand with a wariness that proved wise when the strength of his grip turned out to be even greater than she had anticipated. His hand wrapped almost completely around hers, trapping it as he extended the moment of contact beyond politeness into the realm of pure intimidation.

The calluses on his palm as he eased the pressure

created a friction against her softer skin which felt disturbingly familiar. It was like the faint warning buzz she had experienced when touching a faulty electrical socket. Indeed, the very air around him seemed to crackle and carry a whiff of burning. It was as if there was a huge energy source humming inside him, barely restrained by flesh and blood.

He released her slightly maimed fingers, the gold flecks in his eye blowing with a strange satisfaction as she stayed stubbornly where she was, lifting her firm chin, refusing to be daunted by his superior size and strength, or by the unsettling reciprocal hum in her own bones.

Surprisingly, he was first to disengage from the silent duel, turning away to sling himself down in the chair at the desk, stretching his long legs out in front of him. He didn't offer her a seat, just leaned back and regarded her in a way that seemed indefinably possessive. Vivian's blood tingled in her cheeks and she adjusted her spectacles again.

His thin mouth curved cruelly. 'Shall we proceed to the business in hand, then, Miss Mitchell? I take it you followed all the instructions in the fax?'

She thought of the tense drive down, the nerve-racking hours alone in the motel, the wallowing boat...and his helicopter. She set her teeth and nodded.

'Truly a Marvel—an obedient woman,' he punned goadingly, and Vivian's flush deepened with the effort of controlling her temper. 'And, knowing that your company's successful purchase of my land depends on your pandering to my every annoying little whim, of course you followed those instructions *to the letter,* did you not, Miss Mitchell?'

This time she wasn't going to chicken out. She squared her shoulders. 'No. That is, not exactly—'

'Not *exactly?* You do surprise me, Miss Marvel-lous.'

Nerves slipped their leash. 'Will you stop calling me that?'

'Perhaps I should call you Miss Marmalade instead. That would be a more descriptive nickname—your hair being the colour it is… That wouldn't offend you, would it? After all, what's in a name? "That which we call a rose by any other name would smell as sweet"…'

His frivolity was definitely a trap, the quotation from *Romeo and Juliet* containing a baited message that Vivian could not afford to acknowledge without betraying her tiny but infinitely precious advantage.

'As a matter of fact, there's an awful *lot* in a name,' she said, ignoring the lure. 'Mine, for example, is *Vivian* Mitchell—'

Instead of leaping to his feet in justifiable outrage, he rocked his chair on to its back legs with his booted heels, his expression one of veiled malice as he interrupted her confession. 'Vivian. Mmm, yes, you're right,' he mused, in that low, gratingly attractive voice. 'Vivian… It does have a certain aptness to your colouring, a kind of phonetic and visual rhythm to it…razor-sharp edges springing up around singing vowels. I do have your permission to call you Vivian, don't I, Miss Mitchell?'

'Yes, of course,' she bit off, his feigned innocence making her feel like a mouse between the paws of a lion. 'But you requested that *Janna* Mitchell bring you the documents and co-sign the settlement. Unfortunately my sister couldn't come, so I brought them instead. Other- wise, everything is exactly as you asked…'

'She couldn't come?' he asked mildly. 'Why not?'

Having expected a savage explosion of that banked energy, Vivian was once more disconcerted by his apparent serenity.

She moistened her lower lip nervously, unconsciously emphasising its fullness. 'She has flu.'

Janna was also sick with guilt and remorse, and the combination had made her pathetically easy to deceive. As far as her sister or anyone else knew, Vivian's prime motive for taking her place on this trip was her desperate desire to get away from everyone for a while.

'Convenient.'

She winced at the flick of the whip. Not so serene, after all.

'Not for her. Janna hates being ill.' Her younger sister was ambitious. As a newly qualified lawyer, working in Marvel-Mitchell Realties' legal department, she had a rosy future ahead of her, one that Vivian intended to protect.

'Messes up those gorgeous ice-blonde looks, I suppose,' he said, casting a sardonic look at her wild ginger mane.

Vivian froze.

'You knew,' she whispered, feeling momentarily faint. Thank God the masquerade had only been intended to get her inside the door.

'The moment I saw you.'

'But you've never met Janna—or anyone from Marvel-Mitchell,' she said hollowly. 'Until now you've always insisted on dealing through an intermediary—'

'So you decided to be honest, in spite of the fact I might be none the wiser for the deception. I'm impressed.

Or was I supposed to be?' he added cynically. 'Are you always so honest, I wonder?'

'I try to be.' Her tartness reproved his cynicism.

'A neat piece of sophistry. You try but you don't necessarily always succeed, mmm?' His voice hardened. 'You can't have been so naïve as to think I wouldn't investigate the people I do business with? I'm not a fool.'

'I never thought you were.' But she had seriously underestimated his thoroughness.

'I'm sure that Marvel, too, conducted its own investigations into my integrity…?'

It was a question rather than a comment, and Vivian answered it as such.

'Other than maintaining a current credit check, Peter felt there was no need, since we've been buying and selling properties on your behalf for several years without any problems,' she replied curtly. 'In spite of never having met you, Peter considers you a trusted ally. So your personal integrity was naturally taken for granted, Mr Rose.' Her green eyes were wide and innocent as she made the final, pointed statement.

'Call me Nick, Vivian.' His reaction was equal bland innocence. 'Of course, one man's integrity is another man's poison. I don't do business with cheats and liars.'

'Very wise,' she agreed distractedly, unnerved by his mention of poison. Was that supposed to be significant?

'Are you patronising me, Miss Mitchell?' he asked silkily, planting his feet back on the floor and leaning his torso threateningly towards her.

She was jolted out of her unsettling ruminations. 'I prefer to think of it as pandering to your every annoying little whim,' she said sweetly.

There was another small, dangerous silence. He seemed to specialise in them.

He rose, unfolding himself to his full height with sinister slowness.

'Brave, aren't you?' he murmured.

The thin, menacing smile and the burning gold splinters in his eye told her it was not a compliment. 'So... Instead of the lawyer I requested, Marvel-Mitchell Realties sends me a mere receptionist. A suspicious man might take that as an insult...'

'But then, from your investigations you must know I'm not *just* a receptionist,' Vivian defended herself. 'I'm also Peter Marvel's secretary-PA, and for the last eighteen months a full financial partner in the firm. I'm fully authorised to sign cheques and contracts on behalf of Marvel-Mitchell Realties.'

Not that she ever had. Up until now she had been quite happy to be Peter's sleeping partner—well, lightly dozing at any rate. She enjoyed her work and hadn't looked on the investment of her unexpected inheritance in Peter's firm as an excuse to throw her weight around the office, but rather as an investment in their shared future...

Brooding on that sadly faded dream, she didn't notice him moving until a large hand was suddenly in front of her face. For an awful moment she thought his repressed hostility had finally erupted, but instead of the impact of his palm against her cheek, she felt him pull off her spectacles so that his image immediately dissolved into an indistinct blur.

'Oh, please...' She snatched vaguely, but he was too quick for her.

'Salt build-up from all that sea-spray on the boat trip,'

he said blandly, retreating out of her reach. She squinted to see him produce a white square from his pocket and carefully rub the lenses with it. 'They need a good clean.'

He held them up to the light and inspected them before breathing on the glass and polishing some more. 'Pretty strong lenses. You must be extremely short-sighted.'

'I am,' she admitted truculently. She could have pointed out with brutal honesty that he had a few glaring imperfections of his own, but she was too soft-hearted for her own good—everyone said so. Even Peter who was supposed to be madly in love with her, had always been exasperated by her ability to empathise with the opposing point of view in an argument.

'You must be rather helpless without them.'

Was that a hint of gloating in his voice? She squinted harder. 'Not helpless, just short-sighted,' she said flatly.

Unexpectedly he laughed. It was a disturbingly rich sound, unflavoured by bitterness. 'How long have you worn them?'

'Since I was thirteen.'

And never had she been more grateful, for once there were spectacles firmly perched on her nose she found the boys less inclined to stare endlessly at her ever-burgeoning breasts. From a potential sex-pot she had become an egg-head, and even though her marks had been barely average she had managed to cling to the image until the other girls in her class had also started acquiring ogle-worthy figures.

'May I have them back, please?' she asked the blurry male outline, holding out her hand.

There was a pause. All he had to do was clench those strong fingers and the fragile frames would be crushed, leaving her more vulnerable than ever.

'Of course.'

Instead of handing them to her, he replaced them himself, taking his time as he set them straight across the bridge of her nose, his face jumping back into disturbingly sharp focus, a close-up study in concentration as he tucked the ear-pieces carefully into place, his rough finger-pads sliding around on the ultra-sensitive skin behind her ears for long enough to make her shiver.

'Th-thank you,' she said reluctantly, edging back.

He followed her, his fingers still cradling the sides of her skull. 'You have very speaking eyes.' God, she hoped not! She blinked to clear her gaze of all expression and shuddered again at the intensity of his inspection. What was he searching for?

'Are you cold?'

'No.' To her dismay it came out as a breathy squeak.

His hands dropped to her taut shoulders, then lightly drifted down the outsides of her arms to her tense fists.

'You must be, after being out in that draughty old boat,' he contradicted. 'Your hands are as cold as ice and you're trembling. You need some food inside you to warm you up.'

She cleared her throat. 'I assure you, I'm perfectly warm,' she said, pulling her hands away. 'And I'm not hungry.'

'Your stomach still feeling the effects of the trip?' he murmured with annoying perception, his dark brown eyebrows lifted, the one above the eye-patch made raggedly uneven by the indent of the scar. 'It's a mistake to think the ride back will be easier on an empty stomach. You'll feel much better with something inside you.'

Like you? The wayward thought popped into her head and Vivian went scarlet.

He stilled, looking curiously at her bright face and the horrified green eyes that danced away from his in guilty confusion. What in the world was the matter with her?

His eyebrows settled back down and his eyelid drooped disguising his expression as he took her silence as assent. 'Good, then you'll join me for lunch…'

'Thank you, but the boat leaves again in—' Vivian looked at her watch '—twenty minutes, and I still have to get back down to the wharf—'

'The captain won't leave until he's checked with me first.' He effortlessly cut the ground from under her feet.

'I'm really not hungry—'

'And if I said that I hadn't eaten since lunch yesterday and was far too ravenous to concentrate on anything but feeding my appetite?'

Your appetite for what? thought Vivian as she silently weighed up her options…which proved to be extremely limited.

'I'd say *bon appétit*,' she sighed. Maybe he'd be easier to handle on a full stomach.

'On the principle that it's better I take bites out of food than out of you?' he guessed wolfishly, coming a little too close to her earlier, forbidden meanderings.

'Something like that,' she said primly.

'While I arrange something suitably light for you and filling for me, why don't you get those papers out so I can look them over?'

Looking them over was a long way from signing, but Vivian hastened to do as he instructed while he was gone. He had shut the door behind him, and opened it so quietly on his return that she wasn't aware of him until he loomed over her at the desk. The first she knew of him was the hot, predatory breath on the back of her neck.

'You move very quietly—' she began, in breathless protest at his consistent ability to surprise her.

'For a cripple?' he finished with biting swiftness.

'That wasn't what I was going to say!' she protested, sensing that sympathy was the last thing he would ever want from her.

'You were going to use a more diplomatic term, perhaps?' he sneered. 'Disabled? Physically challenged?'

She was suddenly blindly furious with him. How dared he think that she would be so callous, let alone so stupid, as to taunt him, no matter what the provocation!

'You move quietly for such a *big* man is what I was going to say before you rudely interrupted,' she snapped. 'And an over-sensitive one, too, I might add. *I* didn't leap down *your* throat when you drew attention to the fact I was blind as a bat, did I? And I have two supposedly undamaged legs and yet I never seem to be able to coordinate them properly. I dreamed of being a ballerina when I was a girl…' She trailed off wistfully, suddenly remembering who it was she was confiding in.

'A ballerina?' He looked at her incredulously, his sceptical eye running over her five-feet-ten frame and the generous curves that rumpled the professional smoothness of her suit.

'It was just a childish thing,' she said dismissively, inexplicably hurt by his barely concealed amusement.

He tilted his head. 'So you dreamed of becoming a perfect secretary instead?'

'I wasn't qualified for much else,' she said coldly.

Academically she had been a dud, but she was responsible and willing and got on well with people, her final-year form-teacher had kindly pointed out to her concerned parents, and weren't those things far more important in attaining happiness in the wider world than the mere possession of a brilliant brain?

Of course some people—like Janna and their younger brother, Luke, who was a musical prodigy; and her mother and father, an artist and a mathematician respectively—managed to have it all...good looks included. Not that her family ever consciously made her feel inadequate. Quite the reverse—they sometimes went overboard in their efforts to convince her that she belonged, that she was the much-loved special one of the family. The Chosen One—because she had been adopted as a toddler, and had proved the unexpected catalyst for the rapid arrival of a natural daughter and then a son.

'No other thwarted ambitions?'

'No.' She didn't doubt he would laugh like a drain if she told him that her greatest desire was to be a wife and mother. It was her one outstanding talent: loving people—even when they made it very difficult for her. Sometimes almost impossible.

She looked down at the documents on the desk, concentrating on squaring them off neatly, aware of a nasty blurring of her eyesight that had nothing to do with foggy glasses.

The papers were suddenly snatched out of her fingers. 'This is what you want *me* to sign?'

'Mmm?' Distracted by her thoughts, she took no notice of the faint emphasis. 'Oh, yes.' She pulled herself together, certain that her ugly suspicions were correct and that he was now going to announce dramatically that he had no intention of doing so.

Four months ago, when Nicholas Rose had signed a conditional agreement to sell his Auckland property, his lawyer had cited tax reasons for his client wishing to retain legal title until the end of April. Peter had been happy with the extended settlement date, for it had given him time to chase up the other parcels of land that had been part of the lucrative contract Marvel-Mitchell had entered into with a commercial property development company. Nicholas's property had been the most critical, being a corner lot at the front of the planned shopping mall development, providing the only street access to the larger site. With that in his pocket, Peter had felt free to bid up on one or two other lots, whose owners had demanded much more than current market price.

Then Nicholas Rose had suddenly cancelled his appointment to sign the settlement in Auckland, citing a clause in the conditional agreement that gave the vendor the right to choose the time and place, and Janna had got sick, and Vivian had tried to be helpful and discovered two appalling truths: one, that Nicholas Rose was potentially an implacable enemy, and two, that her cosy dream of love and babies with Peter was shattered beyond redemption.

For long minutes there was no sound but the quiet swish of paper turning, and Vivian's heart thundered in her ears as she waited for her enemy to reveal himself.

'Where do I sign?' He flicked cursorily back through the pages. 'Here? Here? And here?'

'Uh...yes.' He bent and she watched disbelievingly as he uncapped a fountain pen and scrawled his initials in the right places, ending with a full, flourishing signature. The solid gold band on his ring-finger caught her eye as his hand paused, and she stared at the etching of snake and rose, the same crest that she had seen on the letterhead in his lawyer's office.

'Now you.'

She numbly took his place as he stood aside. The shaft of the expensive pen was heavy and smooth, warm from his touch, and she was so nervous that she left a large blob after her name. He blotted it without comment.

'We'll need this properly witnessed, won't we?'

He didn't wait for an answer but went to the door and bellowed for 'Frank'.

The man in the dark suit came in. He gave Vivian a single, hostile, sharply assessing look, then took the proffered pen and co-signed the document with a tight-lipped frown.

'Satisfied?' he asked gratingly as he straightened up, throwing the pen down on to the desk.

'Thank you, Frank.'

Frank grunted.

'Lunch ready?' Nicholas Rose asked, seemingly undismayed by his employee's surly air of disapproval.

'In the kitchen. Just as you ordered, *sir.* Just don't expect me to serve it!'

'We'll serve ourselves.' He turned to Vivian, who was watching the by-play with slightly dazed green eyes, still stunned by the inexplicable reprieve. Could she have been wrong about him, after all? 'Frank heats up a mean soup. Frank is my right-hand man, by the way. Frank, this is Vivian.'

Another grunt and a bare acknowledgement.

'I think Vivian has something to give you before you go, Frank.'

'I do?' She looked at them both blankly.

'The money, Vivian,' Nicholas reminded her helpfully. 'If you haven't brought the cash and the bank-cheque, then this contract of sale isn't worth the paper it's written on.'

'Oh!' She blushed. How unprofessional. She was surprised he hadn't asked to see the money earlier. 'Oh, yes, of course. It's right here.'

She unfastened a locked compartment of her satchel, drawing out the thousand-dollar bundle of notes from a cloth bank-bag, and the crisp slip of paper that made up the balance. She was about to put them down on the desk when she hesitated, eyeing the settlement papers still splayed out in front of him, her fears blossoming anew. Her colour drained away as she nibbled her lip.

With a sardonic look, Nicholas Rose silently gathered up the papers and handed them to her. She tucked them hastily into the satchel before she gave him the bundles. She couldn't quite hide her relief at getting rid of the oppressive responsibility and was chagrined when he tossed the money casually to Frank, who stuffed it in his suit pockets and stumped out, muttering something about the pilot.

'This is all very unorthodox,' she said disapprovingly.

'I'm a very unorthodox man.' If that was a warning, it had come far too late to be of any protection. 'Did it make you nervous travelling with such a large sum of cash?'

She thought of her sweaty drive and the almost sleepless night in the motel with a chair propped under the doorknob. 'Very.'

'Poor Vivian, no wonder you look so pale and tense.' He casually brushed her cheek with his thumb and she nearly went through the roof at the bolt of electricity that sizzled her senses.

They looked at each other, startled. His gaze dropped to her soft naked mouth, open in shock, then to the sliver of thickly freckled skin revealed by the modest cleavage of her blouse and the faint suggestion of lace hinted at by the trembling rise and fall of her lush breasts against the cream silk. In that single, brief glance he stripped her naked and possessed her.

'Come into the kitchen,' he said quietly. 'I know just what to give you to relax.'

He ushered her before him and she moved awkwardly, shaken by the most profoundly erotic experience of her life. And yet he had scarcely touched her! She felt confused, fearful and yet achingly alive, aware as never before of the feminine sway of her full hips and the brush of her thighs beneath her skirt. Her spine tingled in delicious terror. Was he stroking her again with that spiky look of hunger? Imagining how she would look moving in front of him without her clothes? She blushed in the dimness of the hall and chastised herself for her dangerous fantasies. Either it was all in her own mind, or Nicholas Rose had decided to set her up for a very personal form of humiliation. He couldn't possibly be genuinely attracted to her, not a man who, despite his physical flaws, possessed a raw magnetism that probably gave him his pick of beautiful women, not a man who showed every sign of being bent on vengeance.

The kitchen was small and compact and clearly the preserve of someone who enjoyed cooking. The benchtop was wooden, slicked with the patina of age, in contrast to the microwave and modern appliances, and in the small dining-alcove was a well-scrubbed kauri table and three chairs. Evidently Nowhere Island was not normally used for business entertaining.

The table was set with rush place-mats and solid silver cutlery, and the steaming bowl of thick, creamy, fragrant soup that was set before her made Vivian's tense stomach-muscles uncoil. There were bread rolls, too, which Nicholas got from the microwave, cursing as he burnt his fingers on the hot crusts.

The relaxant turned out to be a glass of champagne. And not just any old bubbly, but Dom Perignon. Vivian watched as he deftly opened the wickedly expensive bottle over her murmured protests that wine in the middle of the day made her sleepy, and turned his back to pour it into two narrow, cut-crystal flutes he had set on the bench.

Vivian drank some more soup, and when she was handed the chilled flute with a charming flourish accepted it fatalistically.

'Have you ever tasted Dom Perignon before?' he asked, seating himself again, and this time applying himself to his soup with an appetite that definitely wasn't feigned.

'Why, yes, I have it every morning for breakfast, poured on my cornflakes,' she said drily.

'You must be a lively breakfast companion…albeit a more expensive one than most men could hope to afford,' he said, with a provocative smile that was calculated to distract.

But not you. It was on the tip of her tongue to say it, but she manfully refrained. 'I pay my own way.'

His eyes dropped to her hand, nervously tracing the grain of the table, and the smile was congealed.

'Yes, that's right, you do, don't you. Even to the extent of bank-rolling your fiancé's grand property schemes. I suppose you could say he gained a sleeping partner in more than one sense of the word…'

As she gasped in outrage, he lunged forward and trapped her left hand flat on the table-top, his palm pressing the winking diamond ring painfully into her finger.

'You've been working for him since you left school, haven't you? What took him so long to realise you were the woman of his dreams? It was around about the time you got that little windfall, wasn't it? Did he make it a condition of his proposal that you invest your inheritance in his business, or did you do it all for love?'

'How dare you imply it had anything to do with money?' she said fiercely, fighting the sudden urge to burst into pathetic tears and throw herself on his mercy. 'Peter asked me to marry him before he ever knew about the trust!' The release, on her twenty-third birthday, of funds from a trust set up by her natural parents had been a surprise to everyone, including her adoptive parents, who had refused to accept a cent of it. It was for Vivian to use how she wished, they had said—so she had.

'The wedding's this Saturday isn't it? Your twenty-fifth birthday?'

Her eyes lowered, her hand curling into a white-knuckled fist as she pulled it violently from under his and thrust it down into her lap. His investigations must have been appallingly extensive. How much more did he know? Please God, not enough!

'Yes.'

Her curt response didn't stop his probing as he leaned

back again in his chair. 'You must be looking forward to it after such a very long engagement? And only four days to until death do you part. No wonder you look slightly…emotionally ragged. It's going to be a big church wedding, I understand. I'm amazed you could spare the time to dash down here…or was this a welcome distraction from the bridal jitters?'

Vivian lifted her chin and gave him a look of blazing dislike. At the same time she lifted her champagne glass and took a defiant sip.

He watched her with a thin smile, and suddenly she had had enough of his subtle tormenting. Any moment now she was going to lose her temper and give the game away. Thinking, In for a penny, in for a pound, she closed her eyes and recklessly quaffed the whole lot. It really was glorious, like drinking sunshine, she decided, drenched in a fizzy warmth that seemed to invade every body-cell.

She was still feeling dazzled inside when she re-opened her eyes and found him regarding her with serious consternation.

'You shouldn't knock Dom Perignon back like water!'

Well, she had certainly succeeded in changing the subject! She gave him a smile that was almost as blinding as her hair. 'I thought that was the way you were supposed to drink champagne. It gives such a delicious rush! I think I'll have some more.' She held out her glass.

His jaw tightened. 'One glass is more than sufficient for someone who claims not to drink very much.'

'But I like it. I want another one,' she insisted imperiously. 'A few minutes ago you were trying to ply me with wine, and now you're sitting there like an outraged vicar. More champagne, garçon!' she carolled, waving the glass above her head, suddenly feeling marvellously irresponsible. She might as well get thoroughly drunk before she met her fate.

'Vivian, put the glass down before you break it!' he ordered sharply.

'Only if you promise to fill it,' she bargained, crinkling her eyes with delight at her own cunning.

He looked at her silently for a moment, during which her body began to take on a slow lean in the chair. 'All right.'

She chuckled at him. 'You promise?'

'I promise.'

'Cross your heart and hope to die?'

'Vivian—'

'Stick a needle in your eye—!' She broke off the childish chant, putting her free hand to her open mouth, her face blanching under the freckles. 'Oh, God, Nicholas, I'm sorry.'

'The glass, Vivian—'

She was too shocked at her thoughtlessness to register anything but her own remorse. 'Oh, Nicholas, I didn't mean it, I was just being silly. You mustn't think I meant—'

'I know what you didn't mean, Vivian,' he ground out, as she regarded him owlishly from behind her spectacles.

'I would never tease you about your eye,' she whispered wretchedly.

'I know,' he said grimly, lunging to his feet and reaching for her glass just as her limp fingers let it go. It slid past his hand and shattered on the stone-flagged floor into hundreds of glittering shards.

'And now I've smashed your lovely crystal,' she said

mournfully, her eyes brimming with more tears at the knowledge of the beauty she had carelessly destroyed. 'You must let me buy you another one.'

'By all means pay for the glass. You've smashed a hell of a lot worse in your time. Perhaps it's time you were made to pay for that, too,' he growled, and caught her just as she toppled off the chair, bumping her cheekbone on the edge of the table.

'Oh!' Her back was arched across his knee, her head drooping over his powerful arm, hands flopping uselessly to the floor. 'You've gone all wavy and soft,' she murmured dizzily.

'Your glasses have fallen off.' His voice came from such a long way away that she had to strain to hear it. Her thoughts seemed to flow stickily through her head, oozing aimlessly like melted honey and slurring off her tongue.

'Why won't my arms move? What's happening to me?'

'Perhaps you're drunk.'

She felt a warm weight slide under her knees and then the whole world went around and she gave a little cry as she seemed to float up towards the heavy-beamed ceiling.

'I don't think so. I never get drunk.' The rocking feeling didn't make her feel sick as the boat had. She was being carried, she realised muzzily, struggling against the dragging desire to melt into the arms that held her against a hard chest.

'What's happening, where am I going?' she slurred weakly.

'Wherever I care to take you,' came the terse reply. 'Don't you know what you've done, Vivian?'

She had used to know, but somehow the knowledge was now wispily elusive. 'No, what have I done?' she mumbled.

'You've pricked yourself on a thorn, a very dangerous kind of thorn...'

'Poison.' The word floated up through her subconscious without fear. 'Was it poisonous? Am I dying now...?' It was much nicer than she expected, she decided woozily, aware of a strange, shining whiteness all around.

'No, damn it, you're just going to sleep. You're only drugged, not poisoned.'

'Must've been a rose-thorn, then,' she said, having trouble getting her silly tongue around the words. There was a flat, echoing, metallic rhythm coming from somewhere close by, keeping time with the rhythmic rocking that was making her float higher and higher away from reality. Confusing images clouded in her wandering brain. 'Was a rose, wasn't it...tha' caused all th' tr'ble? In B-Beauty an' the Beast...'

'You're getting your fairytales mixed up. Sleeping Beauty.' The bitter steel of his voice cut into her fading consciousness. 'I may be a beast but my name's not Rose—it's Thorne, Nicholas Thorne.' His grip tightened and he shook her until her bewildered green eyes opened, staring fiercely down at her.

'You do remember my name, don't you, Vivian?' he burst out harshly. 'Even if you never saw my face. Nicholas Thorne. The man you almost destroyed ten years ago. The Olympic athlete whose future you smashed to bits with your car?'

She stirred weakly in his arms. 'No...!'

'The man whose wife and son died while you walked away with hardly a scratch,' he went on relentlessly. 'Do you believe in the Bible, Vivian? That justice is an eye for an eye...?'

She rejected the horror of what he was implying, the black eye-patch suddenly dominating her hazy vision. Perhaps he intended that it was the last thing she would ever see! Frantically she tried to bring her hands up to hide her face, to protect her eyes from his avowed revenge, but they, like the rest of her body, refused to respond to orders.

'*No!*' She was falling now, with nothing to save her. He had thrown her from the high place into a pit of horror. She was falling down, down, down and he was falling with her, his breath hot on her face, his unmasked hatred and the formidable weight of his hard body pressing her deep into the soft white oblivion that was waiting to receive them.

'Ssh, I've got you.'

Her body twitched feebly. '*No...*'

'Fight it all you like, Vivian, it's too late,' he murmured in her ear, with the cruel tenderness of a murderer for his victim. 'All you're doing is hastening the drug's absorption into your system.' His hand was heavy across her throat, his thumb pressing against the sluggish pulse under her jaw as his voice deepened and roughened 'You may as well accept that for the next few hours I can do whatever the hell I like with this voluptuous young body and you won't be able to lift a finger to stop me. Would Marvel want you back, I wonder, if he knew that someone else had grazed in these lush pastures?'

Strangely, the lurid threat with its menacingly sexual undertones didn't terrify her as it should have. To be ravished by a man who could make her tingle all over with just a look didn't seem such a bad thing. She was sorry she would miss it. She might even have said as much, for as her eyelids seeped closed for the last time she heard a soft, incredulous laugh.

Her last conscious awareness was of his mouth warm on hers, his tongue sliding intimately into her moist depths, a leisured tasting of her helplessness as large hands began smoothing off her clothes.

And the sound of someone wishing her sweet dreams.

CHAPTER FOUR

WHEN Vivian opened her eyes she was still trapped in the fuzzy white wilderness.

She blinked, and discovered that she was lying in an incredibly soft, warm bed and the whiteness was the curving surface of a wall a few inches from her nose. She reached out to touch the rough plaster surface, using the contact with reality to push herself upright, meaning to peer out of the narrow window which broke the curve of the wall at the end of the bed. Instead she sank back on her heels with a smothered moan as her head swam horribly.

'Poor Vivian. Head thumping like a drum?'

She opened herself mindlessly to the warm sympathy in the sugar-coated voice. 'Umm…' she groaned in inarticulate agreement.

The sugar melted to sickly syrup. 'Hangovers are a bitch, aren't they? I had no idea you were such a reckless drinker. I told you champagne shouldn't be knocked back like water…'

Vivian swung around on her knees and froze, uttering a gasp of shock as she discovered why the bed was so blissfully warm.

'You!'

'Who did you expect? The faithful fiancé?'

Nicholas Thorne was sprawled beside her, his solid outline under the covers blocking the only escape-route from the narrow single bed. His tanned shoulders were dark against the stark white pillows and his chest above the folded sheet bare, apart from a thick dusting of gold-flecked body-hair that didn't soften the impact of the powerful slabs of raw muscle. Even lounging indolently in bed he managed to exude an aura of barely leashed strength. His head was propped against the stout slats of the wooden bed-head and, with his tousled blond hair and scarred beauty, and a mockingly cynical smile on his lips, he looked to Vivian like the epitome of sin—a fallen angel begging for the redemption of a good woman...

It was a shockingly seductive thought and she wrenched her eyes away from their forbidden fascination with his body, all too aware that his expression of sleepy amusement was belied by the tension in the muscles of his arms innocently resting on top of the bedclothes, ready to thwart any foolish lunge to freedom across his body. Not that she was in any condition to make one. She could hardly think, over the riot in her head. She rubbed a hand across her aching eyes and gasped, suddenly realising what was so different about him. He wasn't wearing his eye-patch.

'You have two eyes!' she blurted out.

'Most people do,' he said drily. 'But, in my case, one is strictly non-functional.' He angled his head so that she could see the immobility beneath the distorted left eyelid, the clouded iris.

'H-how did it happen?' she whispered shakily.

'You have to ask?'

She closed her own eyes briefly. 'Yes, it seems I do. They told me at the time that your injuries weren't serious—'

'I find that hard to believe.'

Her eyes flew open at his harsh scepticism. 'I was only fifteen! Still a minor as far as the law was concerned— nobody told me very much of anything. The police dealt mostly through my parents—' She broke off, realising the dangers of her impulsive self-defence. 'But you can't blame Mum and Dad for wanting to protect me,' she protested quickly. 'They were just doing what any parents would have done in the circumstances...'

In fact, they had been so anxious that she should not be traumatised by the tragedy that they had shielded her from all publicity surrounding the accident, and most of her concrete information had come from that dreadful night at the hospital where, still in a state of shock, she had been gently questioned by a Police Youth Aid officer. She was told that the pregnant front-seat passenger of the other car, Mrs Barbara Thorne, had been thrown out and killed instantly when it rolled down a steep bank. The driver, Nicholas Thorne, had suffered concussion and leg injuries. His son, who had been belted into a back seat, had also miraculously escaped without life-threatening injury.

The car-load of boisterous teenage party-goers, including fourteen-year-old Janna, that Vivian had been driving home along the gravelled country road had suffered only shock and bruises.

To her relief he didn't pursue the point. Instead he stroked a finger across his scarred lid and said simply, 'Fragments of flying glass. This was slashed to ribbons, although fortunately my sight seemed to have suffered only temporary damage. But an infection set in a few months later. A microscopic sliver of glass had worked its way through to the back of the eye…'

And here she was moaning in self-pity over a mere headache! 'And…your leg?'

'Not as bad as the limp might suggest. I can do pretty well everything on it that I used to.'

'Except run.'

Several days after the tragedy she had overheard part of a low-voiced conversation between her parents in which her father had said it had been a twin celebration for the Thornes that night—Nicholas's twenty-fifth birthday and the announcement that his sprinting had earned him selection to the New Zealand Olympic team.

'Oh, I can still run. Just not like a world-class sprinter,' he said, in a voice as dry as dust.

'I see…' She might as well plough on and remind him of *all* the dreams that meeting her on a rainy road that night had crushed. 'And…you never married again?'

'No.'

The clipped reply said more than all the rest. 'I'm so sorry,' she said, her voice crushed with guilt and compassion.

His expression tightened dangerously, then relaxed as he studied her gravity, the sincerity of the pain-glazed green eyes and tragic freckled nose. His gaze flickered over her kneeling figure, and he smiled with sinister intent that curled her toes.

'How sorry, I wonder?'

'Wh-what do you mean?' She put a hand up to her pounding head, overwhelmed by the impossibility of dealing with his unpredictability in her debilitated state. One moment he seemed charming, almost gentle, the next he was brimming with black-hearted villainy.

Maybe she wasn't even awake yet at all. Maybe this whole ghastly week was just one, ultra-long, insanely bad dream…

'Having trouble concentrating, Vivian?'

'My head…' she muttered, hating herself for showing such weakness in front of him.

'Perhaps you'd like some hair of the dog? Champagne seems to do wonders for your mood. Makes you very… co-operative.'

Vivian stiffened. 'It wasn't the champagne, it was whatever vile stuff you put in it,' she growled raggedly.

'You mean the chloral hydrate?' He met her accusing glare without a flicker of remorse. 'I assure you, it's a very respectable sedative—the drug of choice for a whole generation of spy novels. Hackneyed, perhaps, but very effective: tasteless, odourless, highly soluble and fast-acting. You might feel a little hung-over for a while, but there won't be any lasting physical effects—at least, not from the *drug*…'

She wasn't up to interpreting any cryptic remarks. She was having enough trouble trying to establish the most obvious facts.

'Where am I, anyway?' she croaked, looking around the small, cheese-wedge-shaped room.

'The lighthouse. I'm in the process of having it converted into living-space. In fact, you might say this is the penthouse suite.'

Vivian winced as his words reverberated like a knell of doom inside her fragile skull. She lifted her other hand

and massaged her painfully throbbing temples, desperately trying to remember how she had ended up in bed with her worst enemy—a man who ten years ago had accused her of murder and Janna of complicity, in words that had burned the paper on which they were written with their vitriolic spite.

Her fingers pressed harder against the distracting pain as she asked the question that should have been the first thing out of her mouth.

'What are you doing here?'

'If you mean physically, rather than existentially, at the moment I'm just enjoying the view.'

He wasn't referring to the window behind her, Vivian realised, as his gaze slid several points south of her pale face, where it settled with a sultry satisfaction that made her belatedly aware of a growing coolness around her upper body.

She looked down, and gave a mortified shriek as she saw that her chest was as bare as his—more so, since she didn't have a furry pelt to cloak her firm breasts, thrust into lavish prominence by her unconsciously provocative pose. All she had to hide behind were her freckles, which were scant protection from his mocking appraisal. In the split second before Vivian whipped her arms down, she was shamefully aware of a tightening of her pointed nipples that had nothing to do with the invisible caress of chilled air.

Flushed with humiliation, she snatched at the bedclothes, tugging the sheet up to her face as she cringed against the rough wall behind her. Outrage burned away her drug-induced lethargy as her blush mounted. All the time that they had been talking, Nicholas Thorne had *known* that Vivian was unaware of her semi-nudity. While she had been seriously struggling to communicate, he had been encouraging her to flaunt herself like a floozie, savouring the anticipation of her inevitable embarrassment!

She skimmed an exploring hand down under the covers and found to her deep dismay that all she had on were her tiny bikini panties.

'What happened to my clothes?' she demanded furiously, sweeping a blurred look around the room. The bed, a small bedside cabinet and a strange, triangular clothes-horse in the centre of the room appeared to be the only furniture. No closet or clothes, masculine or feminine, appeared in evidence.

'Don't you remember taking them off?' he asked, shifting to fold his arms casually behind his head, his leg brushing her knee under the covers and making her jump.

'No, I do not!' she gritted back fiercely. 'I remember *you* taking them off.'

Her fingers tightened their grip on the sheet, her eyes blazing green fury above the white veil of cotton as it all came rushing back in vivid detail. He had been kissing her, gloating over her helplessness, and it was only because of his insidious drug that she hadn't fought him tooth and claw!

But she wasn't helpless now, she thought grimly. He wanted a run for his money and that was what he was going to get!

After all, that was the reason that she had knowingly walked right into the jaws of his meticulously baited trap.

Her plan was beautifully simple: by presenting Nicholas Thorne with his prime target at point-blank range, she would draw his fire long enough to exhaust or at least appease the machiavellian lust for vengeance that was compelling him to treat anyone and anything that Vivian loved as a pawn to be used against her.

'Did I?' His surprise was patently mocking. 'Goodness, how shocking of me. Are you sure it wasn't just a wishful fantasy?'

'The last person I would want to fantasise about is *you!*' She whipped the sheet down to her chin, raking him with a look of furious contempt. She was prepared to take anything he dished out, as long as he left her family alone. The success of her whole mission hinged on his never finding out that she was a willing self-sacrifice.

'You lured me here under false pretences. You drugged me and took off my clothes!' she hissed at him goadingly.

'Only the ones that were superfluous to requirements,' he replied blandly.

'What in the hell do you mean by that?' She bristled like a spitting ginger kitten, all kinds of wild scenarios exploding through her scandalised imagination.

'What do you think I mean?' He stretched the arms behind his head languidly, expanding the impressive structure of his chest as he murmured tauntingly, 'Are you wondering whether those sexy emerald-green panties are a tribute to my gentlemanly honour…or to my sexual ingenuity?'

Since it happened to be exactly what she was thinking, Vivian reacted furiously. 'In the circumstances, I hardly think the question of *honour* arises,' she said scathingly.

'You may be right,' he stunned her by replying. He came up on one elbow and Vivian reflexively jerked the covers more securely around her.

Unfortunately, her hasty movement tugged the coverings away from the other side of the bed, exposing Nicholas's long, muscled left flank, lean hip and rippling abdomen. The skin was slightly darker on his half-raised leg and thick torso than on his hip, the naked swimsuit line jolting her with the knowledge that, while she might be semi-nude, he was totally naked!

Thankfully his modesty was preserved by a vital fold of sheet, for Vivian's wide-eyed attention lingered for a startled moment before being hurriedly transferred to his face.

'Some parts of me are fortunately still *extremely* functional,' he purred, his undamaged eye glinting with a predatory amusement. 'Especially in the mornings…'

'Mornings?' Vivian's hot face swivelled gratefully away from him towards the soft yellow-pink glow at the window. 'But…it's sunset,' she protested in weak confusion. 'It's just getting dark…'

'Actually, it's getting light,' he corrected. 'That window faces east, not west.'

Vivian sucked in a sharp breath as the full implication of what he was saying hit her. She hadn't just lost a mere hour or two. She had already spent half a day and a whole night entirely at his mercy!

'Quite so,' he said softly. 'This is the morning after, Vivian. Which, given the fact that we're in bed together, naturally poses the deeply intriguing question: the morning after *what?*'

Vivian stared at the thin, sardonic curl of his mouth that hinted at depths of degradation she hadn't even considered.

'Oh, my God, what have you done?' she whispered fearfully, her body shivering with the disgraceful echo of a half-remembered thrill.

'More to the point, what *haven't* I done?' he murmured wickedly, pivoting on his elbow in a fluid flow of muscle to retrieve something from the bedside cabinet behind him.

He offered it to her and, when she refused to let go of her flimsy shield of bedclothes, let a cascade of coloured rectangles spill on to the rumpled fabric between them. Her back glued protectively against the wall, Vivian frowned stiffly down, afraid to move, and frustrated that the surface of the bed was just beyond the range of her near-sighted focus.

'Here, perhaps these will help.' He sat up in a flurry of bedclothes, ignoring her automatic cringe as, moments later, he pushed her spectacles on to her wrinkled nose. 'Better?'

It was a hundred times worse! Vivian stared, appalled, at the photographs scattered like indecent confetti over the bed.

'Oh, my *God...!*'

'It's a little too late for prayers, Vivian. Your sins have already found you out. Quite graphically, too, wouldn't you say?'

'How...? I... You—'

He interrupted her incoherent stammering smoothly. 'I would have thought that the *how* was self-evident. There's this clever modern invention called photography, you see...'

The sarcastic flourish of his hand made Vivian utter a soundless moan as she saw that what she had myopically mistaken for a clothes-horse was in fact a tripod, topped with a fearfully sophisticated-looking camera, its lens pointing malevolently at the bed.

'And as for the I and you, well—we appear to be pretty brazenly self-evident, too, don't we? Here, for instance…'

Vivian's hypnotised gaze followed his pointing finger. 'See the way you're arched across the bed under me, your arms thrown over your head in abandoned pleasure…'

Vivian clamped the blankets rigidly under her arms, freeing her trembling hands to try frantically to push his away as he sorted through the collection and selected another.

'But this one is my own personal favourite, I think. So artistic…so erotic…so expressive. Don't you agree that we make a sensuous contrast of textures and patterns? With your ginger-dappled skin and my deep tan, and the way our bodies seem to flow over and around each other…'

Vivian tuned out his honeyed taunts, transfixed by the searing image suspended from his fingers.

She had seen raunchy advertisements for perfume in glossy women's magazines that were more physically re-vealing, but it was impossible to be objective now. The couple in this photograph weren't anonymous models posing for public display. That was *her* caught in an attitude of utter abandon, that was *his* nude body aggres-sively crushing her to the bed. She went hot and cold at the idea that he had somehow tapped into her forbidden desires.

Even as a tiny, clinical voice of reason was pointing out that the alignment of Nicholas's fingers on her hip con-veniently covered the precise area where the thin strip of her bikini panties would be, Vivian was shattered by a sickening sense of betrayal. The pictures lied; they depicted an act of violation, not of love!

She tried to grab the photograph out of his hand and, when he laughed jeeringly and held it out of her reach, she fell desperately on the others, tearing them into meticulously tiny pieces, all the while trying to protect her threadbare modesty with the slipping covers.

He laughed again, making no attempt to stop her wild orgy of destruction beyond retaining safe possession of his avowed favourite. 'There are plenty more where those came from, Vivian. It was a very long, exhausting night...'

'I was unconscious,' she panted, rejecting his sly insinuation. 'Nothing happened—' She stopped, stricken. 'My God, you were going to do this to *Janna?*'

'Actually, the original plan was for someone else to play your sister's partner in sin,' he drawled. 'And when they supposedly disappeared together, with the payment for the land, I would send you photos of the lovers and evidence that they had planned the fraud together. You were supposed to come dashing to her defence on the eve of your own wedding, sadly too late to rescue the contract that your company was depending on, but in plenty of time to negotiate the salvage of Janna's personal and professional reputation—at the price of your own, of course...

'Your arriving in Janna's place sabotaged the exquisite complexity of the plan, but I'm nothing if not flexible. As soon as I saw you, I knew I wanted the privilege of handling you to be purely mine...'

She had already guessed much of it, but the callous detachment with which he outlined the bare bones of the plot was chilling.

She gasped, as an even more horrible thought smacked her in the face. 'Who took the photos? Who else was in here, watching us——?' She broke off, shuddering with humiliation at the thought that Frank had been a flint-eyed witness to her degradation...

'I can promise you, Vivian, you weren't seen or touched by anyone but me.' He took a small black wafer of plastic from the table by the bed and pointed it towards the tripod, pressing a button so that she could hear the electronic whirr as the flash momentarily dazzled her eyes. 'Remote control. It's a state-of-the-art instant camera—the photos only take a few minutes to develop.'

He rolled off the bed and Vivian uttered a choking cry, closing her eyes a fraction of a second too late to deny herself a glimpse of taut male buttocks and hard, hair-roughened flanks.

'Prude.' His mockery singed her burning ears. 'Here.'

She peeped warily through her lashes and relaxed a trifle when she saw that he had pulled on his jeans. He was holding out the thin red sweater he had worn the previous day.

He shook it impatiently at her immobility. 'Come on.' He threw it on the bed. 'Put that on.'

'I want *my* clothes,' she said stubbornly, as she watched him apply his eye-patch, raking his thick, blond-streaked hair over the thin band of elastic that held it in place.

'Then want must be your master.' He put his hands on his hips, legs aggressively astride, a bare-chested pirate. 'Or rather, *I* shall—and as your master I'm quite happy for you to remain without clothes indefinitely. In fact, yes, I rather like the idea of keeping you here naked...' He invited her to consider the notion in a dark, seductive voice, watching her defiance waver. 'Nude, you'd be so deliciously vulnerable, so much easier for me to control...'

With a muttered curse, Vivian snatched the sweater and hastily pulled it over her blushing head, contorting herself to arrange it carefully over the top of the bed-clothes before she let them go. Thankfully, the sweater came to mid-thigh, although she still felt horribly exposed as she crabbed to the edge of the bed and swung her feet tentatively to the floor.

'That colour makes you look like a fire-cracker with a lit fuse.'

The faint suggestion of approval confused her. She was acutely conscious of the scent of him clinging to the sweater, mingling with her own, and of the soft brush of the thin fabric against her bare breasts. She licked her lower lip, and then fingered it nervously. It felt fuller than usual.

'What are you going to do—with the photographs, I mean?'

'Why, there's only one honourable thing *to* do with them.'

Hope flared briefly. 'What's that?'

He plucked her hand from her mouth and mockingly kissed the backs of her fingers.

'Have them delivered to the church on Saturday, of course. Your poor fiancé must be given some reason for being left stranded at the altar!'

His tongue flicked against her knuckles, stroking her with a brief sting of moist fire that distracted her from his bombshell. She jerked her hand away, but not before he had caught her wrist and with a savage twist removed Peter's ring from her finger.

'We'll send this bauble along with the pretty pictures, just to make sure he gets the message that he can't have you.'

He tossed it in the air and caught it, flaunting his possession before thrusting it casually into his pocket.

'You can't do that...' Vivian whispered, her first thought of the havoc he could wreak on an already tense situation; that was, if the wedding hadn't already been cancelled. Had Janna and Peter taken her advice seriously and gone ahead with the arrangements, or were they still stubbornly wallowing in joint guilt and remorse?

'Marvel will never marry you now, Vivian. Learn to accept it.'

'No, Peter loves me!' she declared desperately, jumping to her feet. On one level, at least, it was still true. It was because of his deep affection and respect for Vivian that he and Janna had put themselves through such torture over the past few weeks. Vivian hadn't even been able to maintain a righteous fury over the betrayal, for it was obvious that the guilt-stricken pair had suffered agonies trying to ignore and then deny their love, in order not to hurt sweet, gentle, defenceless Vivian.

She had bluntly told them to stop being so nobly self-sacrificing. The practical thing to do would be to forget the huge hassle of calling off the elaborate wedding-arrangements and returning all the presents, and just switch brides. Janna and Peter had looked so appalled that Vivian had burst out laughing. It had been the laughter more than anything that made her realise that perhaps she wasn't as heartbroken as a jilted woman should be.

So, when the first opportunity had presented itself for her to prove that she wasn't the sweet, gentle, defenceless creature everyone was going to feel sorry for, she had grabbed at it defiantly with both hands.

'Marvel's going to take one look at those pictures and

know it's all over between you.' Nicholas continued his ruthless attack. 'He'll never be able to forget the sight of you burning in your lover's arms—'

'We're not lovers!' Vivian shrieked. 'Those pictures— they're all fakes. You just… You posed me, like a *mannequin*—'

'Did I really, Vivian?' he taunted softly. 'You were very willing. Don't you remember telling me how I made you feel all soft and hot and buttery inside, and grumbling that it wasn't fair you had to miss out on the thrill of being ravished by a sexy villain…?'

'That was the drug talking, not me! There's a big difference between being barely conscious and being *willing*,' she pointed out with smouldering force. 'And— and, anyway—if I… If we *had* done anything…I'd *know*…'

'How?' He seemed sincerely curious.

She practically melted her spectacles with the glare she gave him. 'I just would, that's all,' she said stubbornly.

'Not if I was *very* skilful and very tender, and you were very, very receptive… Not if you were all soft and buttery inside,' he said, in a satin murmur that slithered over her skin.

'Stop it! I won't listen!' she cried childishly, covering her burning ears with her hands. His eyes dropped to the sharp rise of the hem of his sweater as it flirted against her upper thighs, and she hurriedly lowered her arms. 'No one else will listen to your lies, either. They'll believe *me*…'

'But you won't be there to tell them the truth,' he said smoothly. 'You'll be here with me. You don't think I'm going to let you go so easily, do you?'

'But you have to let me leave eventually.' She tried to sound confident.

'*Eventually*, you may find that you don't *want* to leave…'

His insinuating murmur filled her with alarm. What was he suggesting—that he intended to turn her into some kind of…*sex*-slave, addicted to the forbidden pleasure that he could provide?

'You can't keep me imprisoned here forever…' she protested faintly.

He shrugged. 'Who's keeping you prisoner? You came here of your own free will. In fact, you've already sent a fax to your office saying that everything is fine and that you'll be back with the contract the day before the wedding. So don't think anyone's going to come flying to your rescue.'

That much was true. She had been too secretive, too determined to solve the problem herself.

When she had gone to visit Nicholas Rose's lawyer, to plead that her sister's illness made it impossible for her to deliver the settlement papers personally, as arranged, Vivian had been still reeling from what she had discovered on her visit to Janna's flat.

Then she had bumped into a secretary over-loaded with files, and glimpsed among the scattered papers a letter addressed to Nowhere Island—but to Nicholas Thorne, not Nicholas Rose.

Some fast and furious digging for information had brought answers that had shocked her out of her self-pitying depression and sent her charging off in a spirit of reckless bravado.

Only now was she realising how ill-prepared she was

for her mission. Nicholas Thorne had shown no sign so far of being open either to intimidation or to reason.

Vivian swallowed. Damn it, she couldn't afford to let negative feelings undermine the determination that had brought her here!

'Look, I realise that you genuinely feel that you have some justification for hating me, but don't you see that what you're doing is *wrong*. That car crash was an *accident*. The police investigated it thoroughly at the time—'

'Your sister claimed that our car skidded as we came around the corner,' he said neutrally.

'Yes, but Janna wasn't *accusing* you of anything,' Vivian explained eagerly. 'She was just describing what she saw. The police said the skid-marks confirmed that neither of us was speeding…it was just the way the gravel had been shifted by the rain, making the road unstable—an act of God…'

Then she added gently, because she knew the tortuous ways that guilt could haunt the innocent, 'Neither of us was to blame for that night. Not me and not you. We'll never know if we could have prevented it by doing something slightly faster or reacting differently, but being human isn't a *crime*…'

She broke off because he was looking at her extremely oddly. 'You think I blame *myself*?'

She hurriedly changed her tack. 'When I wrote to you back then, I just wanted you to know that I was sorry for the accident…I didn't mean to taunt you with your grief, if that was what you thought. I—I never showed your reply to anyone else. I didn't think you meant those terrible threats. I thought it was just your grief lashing out.

I can't believe you've nursed that mistaken grudge all these years. Surely, for the sake of your son, you should have put the tragedy behind you—'

'My *son?*'

The floor suddenly seemed to heave beneath her feet as Vivian realised what his arrested expression could mean. 'I—I know he was injured, and it's all a bit hazy now, but at the hospital I remember the doctor saying he was a very lucky boy to be in the back seat… H-he *is* still alive, isn't he?'

He nodded slowly. 'Very much so.'

'Oh. *Oh!* That's great!' Vivian's eyes were starry with brilliant relief. 'And…in good health?' she asked, with more restrained caution.

'Excellent.'

She beamed at him. 'I'm so glad for you!'

He cocked his head with an ironic smile. 'So am I.'

'It must have been a terrible experience for a child,' she said, her emotions swinging wildly back to deep compassion.

'At fifteen, you were little more than a child yourself.'

She drew herself up to her full height, once more unsettlingly conscious that the top of her head barely reached his unshaven chin. 'I've always been mature for my age.'

'You like children?' he asked inconsequentially.

'Of course I like children,' she said, bewildered.

'Some women don't.'

'Well, I *love* them,' she said firmly. She lifted her chin defiantly. 'Peter thinks I'll make a great mother.'

His eye narrowed. 'From what you know of me, you should be on your knees begging for mercy, not deliberately going out of your way to annoy me,' he warned with silky menace, and she gasped as his big hand suddenly curled around her throat, applying an uncomfortable pressure to draw her towards him until her breasts rested against his chest.

'Take your own advice, Vivian, and forget the past. You're not going home to marry Marvel; you're not going to have his children or share any kind of future with him...'

His hand tightened under her jaw, lifting her up on to her toes, so that she had to clutch at his thick shoulders for balance, her fingers sliding against his smooth skin.

'I'm your future now. I'm the one who controls your destiny.' She gave a little yip as his free hand slipped under the hem of his sweater to splay warmly across her quivering, tautly stretched belly. 'And I'm the one who controls your fertility. The first child you'll ever carry in your womb will be *mine*. The first baby to suckle at your breast will belong to *me,* as you will...'

Vivian trembled in shock at the starkly primitive statement of possession and her equally primitive response. Her lips parted soundlessly as his fingertips skimmed under the lacy band of her panties and pressed gently into the fringes of the downy thicket between her thighs.

'Such a fiery little nest... Is it as hot and spicy as its colour suggests? I'll bet it is...' She gave a faint whimper that was stifled by the nip of his teeth against her tender lower lip and his purred praise vibrating over her tongue. 'I bet you're hot and spicy all over when you're in sexual heat, peppered with those delicious freckles and salted with the sweat of your arousal. I look forward to dining on your splendour...' His hand moved up to brush briefly across the silky undersides of her heavy breasts, pausing to discover the betraying tightness of her nipples.

He made a deep sound of male gratification and suddenly released her, stepping back to study with ferocious pleasure her swaying body and her dazed look of sensual confusion.

His chest rose and fell rapidly, his body rippling with arrogant satisfaction as he straightened her glasses, which were fogged and slightly askew.

'You do see the exquisite justice of it, don't you, Vivian? An eye for an eye is such a paltry vengeance for a man of my sensual nature. I prefer a much more intimate, pleasurable and *fruitful* form of revenge...'

CHAPTER FIVE

'LOST something, Ginger?'

Stomping out of the dilapidated old boat-house, which it had taken her half an hour to break into, Vivian stopped dead.

Yes, my sanity, she wanted to say. She must be mad to allow him to play these games with her; crazier still to be enjoying it.

Nicholas Thorne had threatened her in the most elemental way a man could threaten a woman, and yet it wasn't fear that made her heart race and her stomach churn whenever he was near…

She looked up, squinting against the slanting rays of the setting sun.

He was leaning against the corner of the salt-encrusted wooden building, a familiar, infuriating smile of mockery twisting his narrow mouth, an oilskin jacket flapping open over his grey fisherman's sweater and the usual pair of jeans. Somehow she had difficulty picturing him in a conventional suit, yet he must wear one all the time in his role as ruthless head of a sprawling business empire.

'A boat, perhaps?'

'You have to have one somewhere,' she growled, dis-

turbed as ever by his wicked humour. 'You can't live on
an island without owning *some* kind of boat.'

'Feel free to look around,' he replied with another quirk
of his lips.

'Thank you, I will,' she said cuttingly.

She was glad she was muffled up in the bulky knitted
jumper and her green woolen trousers for around Nicholas
she was uncomfortably aware of her body. It was the way
he looked at her—complacement, possessive, *knowing*...

At least she had clothes to cloak her self-conscious-
ness. After staking his nerve-shattering claim on her
womb, Nicholas had calmly directed her to her suit,
blouse and bra lying crumpled under the bed and led her,
clutching them in a bundle, down the iron stairs to the
room below, where she had found her empty briefcase and
the small suitcase she had left back at the motel at Port
Charles. It held only toiletries, her nightdress and a single
change of clothes, but it was enough to give her a slight
sense of false security.

The sweater she was wearing, however, was his, reluctantly accepted as a necessity if she was to tramp around the
island in the blustery weather and not die of exposure. It had
amused him to lend it to her, just as it amused him to follow
her around so that she couldn't just sneak off and *pretend*
to search for an escape, she had *actually* to do it, thoroughly
exhausting herself in the process. He was always hovering,
offering irritatingly helpful suggestions and teasing her with
intriguing little titbits of information about himself that in-
creased her curiosity about him to a dangerous craving.

The more that she found out about him, the more
Vivian's compassionate heart whispered that Nicholas
was basically a good man whose fixation with brutal

revenge was a cry from the wilderness of his frozen emotional landscape. He had found the loss of his beloved wife and unborn child unacceptable, so, in the nature of a competitive man used to winning, he *hadn't* accepted it, and the long years of denial had formed a barrier against natural healing.

In order to save herself, Vivian had realised that she would first have to save him...

'Poor Vivian,' he commiserated. 'Three whole days of scouring every nook and cranny and you still haven't succeeded in finding a way off the island. When are you going to give up?'

'Never!' She pushed past him and began stalking back up the uneven path from the rocky cove.

'Stubborn wench.' He was close on her heels. 'Maybe you should try offering bigger bribes. Frank was quite offended by the low price you put on his loyalty.'

She snorted. His number-one henchman had proved to be predictably incorruptible, but Vivian had known she was expected to go through the motions. She put her nose in the air, and promptly stumbled and teetered on the edge of a sharp, jagged incline.

A powerful arm whipped round her waist, dragging her back against him. Instinctively she reached behind her to clutch at the sides of his coat, her shocked breath rasping in her throat.

'Don't worry, I won't let you go,' he said, wrapping his other arm around her. 'You're safe.'

She felt his face nuzzling into the side of her neck, the stubble of his jaw pleasurably rough against her skin, and for a moment she leaned weakly against him, tempted by his gentleness.

'Safe? That's a laugh! I won't be safe until I get home!'

'Oh, yes, I bet you feel boringly safe with Marvel,' he said mockingly. 'Two years engaged to the man and your dossier says you never stay overnight at his flat. I'd say that indicates a pretty huge lack of excitement on both sides—'

'Just because I'm not promiscuous it doesn't mean I'm sexless!' she flashed from the depths of her insecurity, deeply resenting his familiarity with the private details of her life.

'I don't think you're sexless, just surprisingly unawakened,' he told her smoothly. 'But I wake you up, don't I? You rise so beautifully to the slightest hint of bait. No wonder you're so gullible—you're tough on the outside and marshmallow within. A delicious bundle of contradictions…'

'*You* can talk,' she said, bristling at the gullible label.

'Oh, do you find me delicious, Vivian? I'm so glad it's mutual.' He smiled archly. 'Would you like another sample?'

'No, thank you!' she lied tightly. That searing, sensuous first kiss in his room had also been his last. His dark threats of sexual domination had made her lightning-swift response to his touch all the more shaming, and yet he hadn't pressed his advantage.

Braced for further brutally expert assaults on her deplorably shaky defences, Vivian had instead been left at the mercy of her own fevered imagination. This subtle form of self-inflicted torture had been refined with an added sadistic twist by Nicholas—she was still forced to share his bed every night.

The first night Vivian had searched everywhere, and

been forced to accept that he was telling the truth when he said there were no extra beds. When she had tried to curl up fully-clothed on the couch in the living-room of the keeper's cottage, Nicholas had simply slung her over his shoulder and borne her off to his room in the tower, coolly telling her that she could change into her nightdress in privacy, or he would strip her himself and she could sleep with him naked. She had chosen dignity over humiliation and then lain on her side facing the wall, stiff with mingled rage and agonised apprehension as she felt him get in behind her.

Then—nothing!

He had whispered goodnight, tucked his arm comfortably around her middle, yawned and gone to sleep. She had tried to wriggle out from under his arm, but in sleep he was just as possessive, his hand sinking more securely under her waist, a thick, hair-roughened thigh pushing between her knees to drape over her leg, anchoring her firmly against the bed. Even through her blessedly modest nightgown she could feel the warm shudder of his heartbeat against her back and the firm definition of his manhood pressed against her soft bottom.

Each succeeding night it had taken her longer to fall asleep, and each morning when she woke up in a confusion of blushes it was to find that some time in the night she had turned over and mingled with him in a trusting sprawl of limbs.

To her chagrin he accepted her rejection with a careless shrug. 'I came to tell you that Frank almost has dinner ready,' he said. 'And I've already warned you it's not a good idea for you to be stumbling around out here alone when it starts to get dark. Look what nearly happened just now—'

'That was because you were distracting me. Maybe you did it on purpose,' she goaded, inexplicably angry at him for caring. 'Or maybe you'd like to see me go over a cliff, to be killed by an "accident". That would be rough justice for you, wouldn't it?'

In the waning light his features were blurred into softness, his eye deeply shadowed by his fierce brow. 'Do you really think I brought you here to kill you?'

'I... No,' she admitted truthfully. His declared intent had been to cause her maximum mental suffering and she couldn't suffer if she was dead. 'But we both know there are worse things than dying...'

He moved closer. 'Like bearing my child, you mean? Would that really be a fate worse than death, Vivian? To make love with me and create a new life...?'

The wind snatched her breath away. 'You only said that to frighten me,' she choked. 'I know you weren't really serious—'

'Do you? Just because I haven't mentioned it again?' He captured her gaze with the bold assurance of his glittering brown eye. 'I knew I didn't have to. I knew you were thinking what it would be like to accept me as your lover. Wondering if I would make love with the same passionate intensity with which I seem able to hate. I was giving you time to get used to the idea. After all, there's no real urgency now that you're here, living, eating, sleeping with me. I've waited this long for you...I can wait a little longer...'

A *little* longer? Heat suffused her body at his arrogant sexual confidence. She fought to cool her instinctive response. How could she feel anything but revulsion at his depraved suggestion?

She shivered. 'Surely you wouldn't use force to—to—'

'Not force—seduction,' he said smouldering. 'We both know that there's been some very volatile physical chemistry brewing between us since the moment we met. Why don't you just accept that we were always fated to become lovers?'

Fate again. Wasn't that the very thing she had come here to defy boldly? Vivian shivered once more.

'You're cold—why didn't you say so?' Nicholas scolded her, shrugging impatiently out of his jacket and wrapping her in the heavy oilskin, tucking her chilled hand firmly through his elbow as he escorted her back along the stony path towards the cottage. 'You should have worn the parka I offered you. No sense in cutting off your nose to spite your face. And if you're going to go storming around in a temper, watch out for the wildlife— they have first priority. Nowhere Island is a wildlife sanctuary and part of a maritime park. All these outlying islands are really the tops of drowned hills, and the eroded volcanic tubes that riddle the shore and sea-floor make very rich habitats for marine life.'

'You sound like an environmental tour-guide,' she said grumpily, trying not to respond to the enthusiasm in his voice.

'I should hope my learning is a little more useful than that,' he said drily as he opened the back door. 'As a marine biologist, I don't approve of environmental tourism.'

'What!'

He pushed her stunned figure over the threshold of the kitchen, where Frank was cursing over a sizzling pan.

'You're a property developer!' she accused, as he

whipped his jacket from around her shoulders and hung it on the back of the door.

'I'm also a marine biologist. It *is* possible to do more than one thing with your life, Vivian. One doesn't have to limit oneself to living down to other people's expectations,' he said softly. Was that a dig at her?

He pressed a finger against her jaw, pushing it closed with a slight snap. 'What's the matter, Ginger? Aren't I fitting into your stereotype of a grief-crazed vengeance-seeker?' He stepped away. 'I'm going to have a quick shower before dinner.' The dark gleam of light reflecting off his eye-patch managed to give the startling impression of a wink. 'Feel free to join me if you want to help conserve the tank-water.'

As soon as he was out of the room, Vivian turned to Frank.

'Does he really have a degree in marine biology?'

'Yep. An athletic scholarship in the States.'

She waited but, as usual, further information was not forthcoming.

'You don't talk much, do you?'

'Don't have much to say.'

She would have been offended if she hadn't discovered that he was almost as taciturn in his communications with Nicholas. She hadn't quite worked out Frank's job description yet; he seemed to be a combination of assistant, valet, bodyguard, mechanic—he had already fixed the faulty back-up generator—and chief cook and bottle-washer.

'Where's Nicholas's son?'

He shrugged. 'Ask Nick.'

'He won't tell me. He won't talk about his son at all.

Or his wife.' She gave a little huff of frustration. 'How long have you worked for Nicholas? Did you ever meet his wife? Do you know what she was like?'

That brought the hawkish face around, bearing a hard stare.

'Six years. No. Beautiful.'

It took her a moment to realise he had actually replied to all her questions. She sighed. 'I thought she must have been.'

Astonishingly Frank's dour expression broke up in a grin.

'Nothing like you.'

She scowled. 'OK, OK, you don't have to rub it in. She was so perfect he's never met another woman to match up to her.'

'Is that what he told you?' His grin widened and she studied him with suspicious green eyes.

'What's that supposed to mean?'

He shrugged. 'It's your life—you figure it out.'

And, with that irritating observation, he crouched down to open the oven and stir something inside.

Vivian was about to demand a proper answer when her eyes fell on a bulge in the front pocket of the jacket hanging against the door. She remembered the weight of something bumping against the side of her knee with a vaguely familiar chink as Nicholas had hurried her along. His keys! She had searched all over the lighthouse, but there was one place she hadn't been able to look.

She darted silently over and boldly plunged her hand into the pocket. Fisting the key-ring, she just had time to nip back to the other side of the room before Frank closed the oven and turned around.

'Uh, I think I'd better go and change for dinner,' Vivian said uncomfortably, edging out of the door.

Her heart was in her mouth as she crept down the hall. The plumbing in the lighthouse was still incomplete, so Nicholas would be showering in the cottage bathroom and probably had his fresh clothes with him, which meant he wouldn't need to go back to his room before dinner. Even if he did, the locked room was on the fourth landing, and she would have plenty of time to hear him on the stairs and whip up to the next level to fossick innocently in her suitcase.

The locked door hid exactly what she had suspected: an office. A businessman with Nicholas Thorne's auto-cratic reputation would never trust anyone enough to re-linquish control of his business, even temporarily. She pulled the door softly to, and switched on the light.

There was a computer work-station and various un-identifiable pieces of electronic equipment, and a big desk strewn with papers.

Vivian ignored the wall of shelves lined with jars and tubes of dubious-looking specimens, her heart sinking at the sight of the heavy steel combination-safe on the floor.

She went over to the desk. Only the top drawer was locked and she rifled quickly through the others, finding mostly stationery and files of scientific papers and journals. Nothing that might tell her more about Nicholas the *man*. No stray photographs of his wife or son. No photos of any other kind either...

Adrenalin spurted through her veins and her sweaty hands shook as she unlocked the top drawer and sat down on the big swivel chair behind the desk to reach inside.

The first thing she touched was a small medicine bottle, and her fingers tightened around the amber glass as she picked it up and read the typed label: chloral hydrate. Her soft mouth tightened and she pushed the half-full bottle into her trouser pocket, intending to dump the contents at the first opportunity.

Her heart gave a nervous convulsion when she saw what the drug had been sitting on—the settlement contract, signed, witnessed, dated—intact and still viable…

She lifted it out and weighed it in her hands. But no…even if she took it, where could she hide it? The fact that Nicholas hadn't already destroyed it was surely a hopeful sign. As long as it lay here undisturbed, Marvel-Mitchell Realties still had a future.

She put the contract back, her breath fluttering as she slid it to one side and saw her forlorn dis-engagement ring crowning one very distinctive, disturbingly erotic photograph. She tried not to look at the haunting image, afraid to touch it lest she become further victim to her depraved fascination with Nicholas Thorne.

But where were the others Nicholas had taunted her with? The wedding was supposed to be the day after tomorrow. If only she could continue to stave off disaster until the ceremony was over! She didn't want her wedding-present to Peter and Janna to be a bunch of pornographic photographs and a threat of financial ruin. She could just imagine the poor vicar's face if he caught a glimpse of any of those pictures. She would never be able to hold up her head in church again!

However much she longed to believe that her brief presence here had taken the edge off Nicholas's bitterness, had softened and changed him, she didn't dare take the risk of relying on her increasingly biased judgement where he was concerned. Only when Janna and Peter were safely and securely married would Vivian let herself take the gamble of trusting Nicholas, telling him the truth and hoping that he would justify her faith in his basic humanity.

She scrabbled frantically through the drawer, reaching deep into the back where she found something firmly wedged. She pulled it out.

A cellphone. She flicked a switch. A *working* cellphone.

Civilisation was only a single telephone call away.

The alternatives bolted through her brain in the space of a split second. She didn't have to go through with it. She could call Peter—call the cops. She could cause a scandal. Make a great deal of misery for everyone concerned, but save herself.

And perhaps drive Nicholas out of her life forever...

She let the telephone clatter back into the drawer at the same instant that she became aware of another presence in the room.

She hadn't heard him on the stairs and now she saw why. His feet were bare as he crossed the uneven wooden floor, not making a sound. He wore only a white towelling robe and his hair drifted in damp clumps across his brow.

He was breathing hard. And he was angry.

'Careless of me.' Nicholas leant over and slammed the drawer viciously shut, nearly catching her guilty fingers in the process.

'And even more careless of you to be caught.' He locked it and wrenched the keys out with a violent movement. Vivian slid out of the chair and nervously backed away.

'What were you doing, Vivian?' he demanded harshly, stalking her every move. 'Snooping? Or were you frantic to get to a phone so you could warn Lover-boy?'

The back of her thighs hit the computer table and she pulled her scrambled wits together as he halted, his whole body bunched with furious aggression.

'*No!*' His appearance had rendered her split-second decision redundant, but she wanted him to know what it would have been. 'No. I—I didn't even know there was a phone in here. I was just looking for the photos—the other ones you said you had—'

'I also said you were gullible,' he sneered. 'The only photos I had, you tore up—except for my personal favourite, of course...' He wasn't wearing his eye-patch and even his sightless eye seemed to blaze with sparks of angry golden life as he smiled savagely at her bitter chagrin.

'I was thinking of having it blown up and framed before I send it to Marvel,' he taunted. 'It'll have so much more impact that way. Perhaps I should even call him myself, give him a blow-by-blow account of how much pleasure I got from having his chaste bride-to-be *mounted...*'

She flinched at the crudely insulting *double entendre*. His volcanic rage seemed wildly out of proportion to the condescending amusement, even wry admiration, with which he had greeted her other failed attempts to thwart him.

'OK, OK, so I took the keys because I wanted to steal from you and snoop among your secrets,' she flared, fighting back with her own fortifying anger. 'I thought I might find something I could use to help persuade you to let me go. What's so terrible about that? *You* snooped through *my* life—'

He stiffened, his expression hardening to granite.

'And, tell me—if I suddenly agreed with everything you said? If I handed you your precious settlement contract and said all debts were cancelled—what then? Would you be able to walk away and forget that any of this ever happened? Would you still marry Marvel on Saturday?'

For a heartbeat Vivian ached to be selfish and trust to his sincerity. 'Why don't you let me go, and find out?' she said warily.

She knew instantly that she had made a serious mistake. His jaw tensed and colour stung his cheekbones as if she had delivered him a sharp slap across the face. Oh, God, had the offer been genuine?

'I wouldn't tell anyone, if that's what you mean,' she said quickly, hoping to repair the damage. 'Nobody back home has to know about any of this. It's still not too late—'

'The hell it isn't!' Turning away from her, he jerked his head towards the door and grated, 'Get out!'

Was he ordering her out of the room, or his life? She moved hesitantly past him. 'Nicholas, I—'

He sliced her a sideways glance of fury that stopped the words in her mouth. 'Frank said you were changing for dinner. Don't make a liar out of him.'

Then his voice gentled insidiously. 'And, Vivian…?' Her fingernails bit into her palms as he continued with dangerously caressing menace, 'If I ever catch you here again, you won't find me so lenient. Be very careful how much further you provoke me tonight. I'm in the mood for violence…'

'If I ever catch you here again…' He wasn't sending her away! Vivian was shocked by the turbulence of her relief as she shakily made her way up to the room where she kept her meagre selection of clothes.

Deciding it might be deemed further provocation not to obey his thinly veiled command, she quickly put on a fresh blouse, the cream one she had worn the day of her arrival, and changed her sneakers for her low-heeled shoes. The trousers, she decided with the dregs of defiance, could stay—she could do with their warmth around her woefully trembly knees.

The kitchen had been transformed in her absence. It was no longer a bright, practical workplace; it was a shadowy corner of a private universe, lit only by twin flickering candles set on a table laid for two. A casserole dish sat in the centre, flanked by a bottle of red wine and two glasses. Nicholas, she discovered with an upsurge of her heartbeat, was still wearing his white robe—a spectral white phantom floating at her out of the darkness.

'What happened to the lights?' she asked sharply. 'Where's Frank?'

There was a brief gleam of teeth from the phantom and a movement of his head so that she could see that the dark triangle of his eye-patch was back in place, his vulnerability well-masked. 'I'm conserving generating power,' he said, in a tranquil tone of reason that sent a frisson down her spine. His silky calm was like the eye of a hurricane—she could feel the energy swirling around it. 'And Frank's already eaten. He's in his bedroom. Why? Did you want him for something?'

The innocent enquiry made her seethe. He knew damned well why she wanted a third person present! Frank was no use as a buffer tucked away in his little concrete bunker down the hall.

It was pure nerves that made her blurt out as she sat down, 'I'm not sleeping with you tonight!'

He sat across from her, leaning his chin on his hand so that his face moved forward into the flickering pool of light, his eye gleaming, a tiny candle-flame dancing like a devil in the hot, black centre. 'What's so different about tonight?'

She was hypnotised by the devil. 'It just is, that's all.'

'Do you mean that you're more aware of me as a man than you were last night?' he murmured.

She didn't think that was possible! 'An *angry* man,' she qualified stiffly.

'I've been angry with you before. Usually you just fling my temper back in my teeth.'

'Usually you behave with more self-control.'

His smile was darkly knowing. 'Maybe it's not *my* lack of control that you're worried about. Don't you trust yourself in bed with me any more, little fire-cracker? Afraid I might have lit your fuse?'

Her soft mouth tightened and he laughed softly, reaching across the table towards her. Vivian stiffened, but he was only removing the lid from the casserole.

'You dish up the food. I'll pour the wine.'

'Oh, but I don't know if I like red wine—'

'You'll like this one. It's a gold-medal winner from a vineyard I part-own in Gisborne,' he said, brushing aside her diffidence as he filled her glass. He poured himself a glass, drank half and refilled it, all in the time it took her to ladle some of the steaming casserole on to their plates.

She waited until she had eaten several mouthfuls of food before she took her first sip. In spite of her determination not to react, she was unable to prevent a murmur of surprised pleasure as the full-bodied flavour exploded against her palate, drenching her senses in its heady bouquet.

'You see, you never know whether you're going to like something until you try it. You need to be more adventurous, Vivian, experiment more…'

She didn't like the strange tension in him…nor the dangerous ease with which he broached the bottle as they both pretended to eat. She noticed he had shaved since their confrontation in his office. It had been necessary for him to shave but not to *dress?* She felt a strange thrill of fear.

'Weren't you afraid?' he said disconcertingly, his deep, hushed tone seeming to weave itself into the darkness. 'The only locked room in Bluebeard's castle… Weren't you afraid of the horrors you might find in there when you stole the key?'

'This isn't a castle and you're not Bluebeard,' she said, resisting the powerful vision he was slyly conjuring out of her imagination. 'You've only ever had one wife,' she said deliberately. 'And I'm certainly in a position to know that you didn't murder her.'

He looked at her broodingly over the rim of his glass. 'Ah, yes, my beloved wife. Frank tells me you're curious about her…' Vivian was suddenly certain that Nicholas was building up towards some kind of critical release of the tension that raged in his face, seethed in his restless eye.

'I'm in the mood for violence…'

She rubbed her damp palms surreptitiously against her thighs and felt the forgotten bulge in her trouser pocket.

The idea sprang into her mind full-blown. Her fingers closed around the glass bottle warmed by her thigh.

'I wouldn't mind a drink of water, please.'

He got up, moving with his usual swiftness and precision, and Vivian knew that in spite of the wine he had consumed he was still dangerously alert. It was only his inhibitions that had been relaxed, and thus the bonds that chained his savage inner demons.

The moment he turned away to the sink, she pulled out the chloral hydrate, wrenched off the lid and tried to shake a few drops into his full wine glass, horrified when the clear liquid came out in a little gush.

She didn't have time to get the bottle capped and back into her pocket, and had to thrust it down on her lap as she accepted her glass of water, feeling the remainder of the drug soak into the fabric over her hip as her heart threshed wildly in her chest.

'You wanted to know about Barbara…'

She watched, her green eyes wide with fascinated horror, as he re-seated himself and took a long swallow of his wine before he spoke again. Oh, God, what madness had possessed her? What if she had given him too much and he died?

'The biggest mistake of my arrogant young life…'

Mistake? Vivian was jolted out of her frantic abstraction.

His mouth twisted at her expression. 'You thought it was the love-match of the century? Mis-match, more like.

It was my father's idea. He's an extremely dominating man and I'm his only son, his greatest pride—and his greatest disappointment. We clashed on just about everything. When I came back from university overseas, he was very ill and used some very clever emotional blackmail to pressure me into marriage with his god-daughter. Needless to say, he then miraculously recovered.'

'Then…you fell in love with each other after the marriage?' Vivian said, her thoughts falling into chaos.

'Love was never part of the equation. Like my father, Barbara saw our marriage in terms of status and control. We lived separate lives from the start. She politely endured me in her bed because it was necessary in order to secure her permanent place in the Thorne dynasty— part of her bargain with my father, I gather—and I politely endured for reasons just as selfish, because I wanted nothing to disturb my build-up for the Olympic trials…'

He paused and Vivian held her breath, hoping the fascinating revelations were going to continue.

'Then Barbara told me she was pregnant and I realised just how permanent was the trap my father had planned for me. Except it wasn't—the next day she and the baby were killed…'

He reached for his wine-glass again and Vivian couldn't stop a darting gesture of involuntary protest.

'Oh, no, please don't drink that!' She clumsily tried to knock it out of his hand.

'Why not? Are you afraid I'll pass out on you before I finish baring my soul?' He stopped, his face sharpening as he looked from her stark expression of appalled guilt to his glass, his shrewd brain making the impossible leap in perception.

'My God, is there something wrong with this? *What have you put in my wine?*'

He lunged across the table with a roar, scattering the burning candles, and Vivian's chair crashed over as she jumped to her feet, sending the empty bottle in her lap spinning to the floor.

She didn't wait to see him recognise it. She fled.

She flew down the hall and crashed through the door into the lighthouse in a blind panic, triggering the sensor lights in the stairwell. She was thundering up the stairs before she remembered there were no locks on the doors, nowhere to hide. It was too late now; she could feel the pounding vibration of his mysteriously delayed pursuit through the steel under her flying feet.

He caught her just below the fourth level, not even attempting to stop her but merely gathering her up in his furious momentum, driving her onwards and upwards with the bulldozing threat of his body. Only when they reached the landing of his room did he actually lay a hand on her, catching her right wrist and using their combined speed to swing her away from the stairs and through the doorway, shoving her back against the wall, anchoring her there with the full thrust of his body, slamming his other hand on to the light-switch so that she was exposed to the full glare of his rage.

'How much did you give me?' he snarled, his breath fogging up her glasses, his lips brushing hers in an angry parody of a kiss. 'The whole damn bottle? How *much,* damn you?' He rattled her against the wall.

'I don't know—a little, a teaspoonful, I don't *know!*' she panted desperately. 'I spilled the rest of it, that's why the bottle was empty. I'm sorry, Nicholas, I panicked, you were frightening me…' She was begging now, but she was beyond caring. 'Please, I'm sorry—'

'*Sorry!*' he ground out. He shook his head violently, as if the drug was already beginning to affect him.

'Maybe you should sit down before you fall down,' she said, feeling wretchedly weak herself.

'Maybe I should,' he said thickly. He pulled her away from the wall and dragged her over to the bed, pulling her between his spread legs as he sat down, fumbling in his bath-robe pocket. She felt a cold metallic clasp replace the heat of his hand on her wrist, and looked down just in time to see him snapping the other handcuff around his own wrist.

'My God, what are you doing?' she asked numbly, staring at their shackled limbs. So this was why she had got such a head start on his superior strength and speed. He had gone to get *chains!*

'Making sure you'll be here when I wake up,' he said grimly. '*If* I wake up.'

She shuddered. 'Don't say that! Please, Nicholas, where's the key? You don't need to do this. I promise I'll stay…'

For an answer he fell diagonally back on the bed, throwing his shackled right wrist forcefully out to his side so that she was brought tumbling down on top of him with a soft scream of terror. He pulled off her glasses and tossed them on the floor in a careless gesture that she found paradoxically even more threatening than his violence.

'Nicholas, no…' She struggled to find purchase with her knees against the mattress, conscious that she was straddling him, and the towelling robe was parting over his powerful thighs.

'Nicholas, *yes!*' He pulled her head down, crushing her mouth against his, wrapping his right arm across her back so that her captive arm was forced behind her. He kissed her until she tried to bite him, and then he nudged her face aside with his jaw and sank his teeth into her vulnerable throat. She cried out, struggling weakly as he began to suckle at the bite, murmuring words against her skin that sapped her will and created tiny shocks of pleasure deep in her feminine core. He began to kiss her again, and this time she didn't fight him and the forceful thrust of his tongue gentled to a slow, seductive glide that made her tremble with yearning.

'I may pass out, but not before I've had a taste of you…not before you've given me everything I want…' His mouth moved to the other side of her throat, nibbling and sucking with tender savagery as his hips and thighs began to undulate beneath her. 'I'm going to devour every lovely inch of you…use my lips and teeth and tongue on you in ways that you've never even imagined…brand you all over with my mark so that anyone who looks at you will know you've come from my bed…'

Vivian knew he was talking about Peter. Briefly surfacing from her passion-drugged state, she tried to arch away, but Nicholas shifted his hand from the back of her neck to the front of her silk blouse, slipping his fingers into the prim neckline and ripping it open with a single downward stroke that scattered the pearl buttons like lustrous tears across his chest.

'Nicholas!'

Her gasp was lost in a spasm of violent sensation as he flicked open the tiny plastic catch between her breasts and allowed them to tumble free of the confining lace. The ginger freckles were stretched over their swollen fullness, the soft pink tips swaying against the hard contours of his chest, contracting instantly into tight points that scraped and caught on his own peaked masculine nipples.

His chest heaved and he uttered a harsh sound, violently tilting his hips to roll her on to her side and then her back, hefting her up against the pillows, rising up and over her on his braced hands. In almost the same motion he loosened the belt of his robe so that it fell open around her, baring the full length of his body to her restless gaze. He was hugely aroused and shuddering with a fierce tension, for all the world as if she had given him an aphrodisiac instead of a sedative.

He looked triumphantly down at the lavish bounty he had exposed, his nostrils flaring as he caught the enticing scent of her body, and recognised the subtle signals of her arousal.

'Yes—*Nicholas*,' he ground out. 'Not Peter, *Nicholas*. Admit it. You couldn't give a damn about him when you're with me!'

He cupped her breast with a possessive movement of his manacled hand, the narrow chain connecting their wrists dragging in a cold caress against the skin of her ribs as he moved deliberately, his fingers contracting and relaxing, his thumb rubbing against the rigid nipple.

He bent his head and his tongue darted out to curl around the tip he was cherishing, dragging it up into his mouth, moistening it with tender care then releasing it to the cool night air.

'You don't love him; you don't want to marry him.' The words were muffled by her flesh. 'You don't want to cling to your safe, unadventurous past…you want the fierce ex-

citement only I can give you…you want this…and this…'
He held her pleasure-drenched gaze as his mouth closed
over her, slanted softly, sucked lightly, twisted, lifted and
lowered again…

'I'm…not…the one who won't let…the past go,' she
panted, biting her lip as he repeated the voluptuously un-
satisfying action over and over, clenching her chained
hand helplessly against her side, groaning with sweet
agony as he finally used his teeth and suckled her with the
rough urgency that she needed, marking her as he had
promised with his erotic brand of possession. Her ex-
travagant response made him explode into action, pushing
heavily between her thighs, moving jerkily on her as if the
fabric between them didn't exist, as if he was already
buried deep inside her, pleasuring them both beyond
imagining…

'Say it, Vivian…stop holding yourself back…stop
pushing me away.' She was suddenly aware of a settling
heaviness in his body as his head sank down on her
shoulder. 'Don't let me go down into this damned
darkness without a prayer…'

'Stop talking about dying!' she cried frantically,
tugging at his hair to try and keep him awake.

'I'm not talking about dying. I'm talking about living.
I can't let him get you… Gotta keep you with me,' he said
with a blurred illogicality that Vivian knew from experience was the drug tightening its grip on his mind, but she
sought to drag him back to her with desperate words of
truth.

'Peter won't ever get me because he doesn't *want* me,
damn you. Do you hear me, Nicholas Thorne? You were
right. I don't love Peter and Peter doesn't love me. He

loves my *sister*. It's *Janna* he's going to marry on Saturday, you big, gullible oaf, not me!'

For a moment he remained still, a dead weight, and she thought he had lapsed into unconsciousness, but then he suddenly rolled off her in a tangle of white towelling.

'What did you say?'

The face beside hers on the pillow suddenly looked completely wide awake. But no, his pupil was almost a pinpoint. He was conscious through sheer force of will.

She moistened her lips and nervously tucked her blouse across her breasts one-handed as she said in a husky little voice, 'I cancelled our engagement last week. But not the wedding. You see, I found out Peter and Janna had fallen in love, and, well—they were sort of mired in the inertia of their guilt. They didn't deliberately set out to hurt me, and I realised I hadn't ever really been in love with Peter, not the way that Janna is. So I told her to go ahead and get married in my place and I'd dance at their wedding.'

She smiled to show how bravely she had accepted the crushing blow to her feminine pride, but the smile began to waver under his sombre stare and, to her horror, her eyes began to fill.

'I suppose now you're going to tell me I got what I deserved,' she whispered, and burst into a flood of tears.

But instead of gloating, as she had always dreaded that he would, Nicholas quietly gathered her shuddering body against his warm length and stroked her wild ginger mane, uttering soothing murmurs while she sobbed out all the wretched details against his chest.

It took a long time to expend her storm of stored-up tears, and repeated assurances from Nicholas that he had no interest in wreaking his savage revenge on her damned sister's damned wedding, before Vivian finally hiccupped herself into exhausted sleep. Only then did the man holding her allow his mind and body to go equally lax, finally relinquishing his formidable will to the powerful seduction of the drug in his veins.

CHAPTER SIX

VIVIAN took another frigid slap in the mouth and felt her throat burn with the salty abrasion as she coughed the seawater out of her lungs.

She sluggishly instructed her head to turn and her arms to rise and fall, rise and fall, in the rhythmic stroke that had won several long-distance ocean swims at the surf-club she had belonged to in her late teens.

The wet-suit that she had taken from among the diving-gear in the lighthouse storeroom was providing her with extra buoyancy and some protection against the cold, but she knew that mental stamina would be her greatest asset in the gruelling swim.

She turned on her side, checking that she was still moving in the right direction, heading towards the uneven lurch against the horizon that Frank had let slip one day was the nearest inhabited island. Thank God the weather was good and the sea not too choppy, but even if there had been a cyclone Vivian wouldn't have cared.

She had woken just before dawn and looked at the man lying next to her in a deep, drugged sleep and acknowledged with a thrill of despair that she was in love with her capricious captor.

In the space of a few days the morals of a lifetime had been swept away. Instead of drawing Nicholas into the sunlight of reason, she had been drawn into the shadows. Something dark in herself was called forth by the darkness in him. She could protest all she liked, but all Nicholas had to do was touch her and she melted. And he knew it.

Last night he had admitted that he had never loved his wife. That called into question everything she had come to believe she knew about him. It made his motive for revenge not one of honest emotional torment, which could be appeased, but of cold-blooded, implacable malice.

The realisation that Nicholas must have uncuffed her before he fell asleep was merely confirmation of her bleak theory that he believed he had won their battle of wills. The empty steel bracelet dangling from his own still-manacled wrist was a mute testament to his confidence in her sexual subjugation.

Protest had exploded in her brain. *No!* She wouldn't let him distort her love into something that she was ashamed of. She had to be out of his reach before he woke up. Before he could touch her again...

Fool, fool, fool, Vivian chanted inside her head, in rhythm to her stroking through the water. To believe that you could play with fire and not be burnt. Fool, fool...

'Little fool! What in the hell do you think you're doing? Of all the ridiculous, theatrical stunts!'

She suddenly realised that the new voice was much deeper than the one in her head and far more insulting, and the loud slapping sound wasn't the rising waves hitting her face; it was the sound of oars striking the water.

Water sheeted down her face from her sopping hair, sticking her eyelashes together and getting in her swollen eyes as she stopped to tread water and was nearly run down by a small aluminum dinghy rowing furiously towards her.

Nicholas was shipping the oars, leaning over the side, yelling, cursing, trying to grab her slippery wet-suited arm.

Vivian swam away, coughing and spluttering as she briefly sank. When she struggled to the surface again, Nicholas was standing silhouetted against the crisp morning sky, the boat rocking dangerously. 'For God's sake, Vivian,' he cried bleakly. 'Where in the hell do you think you're going?'

Still choking on salt-water and shock, Vivian didn't bother to answer; she just pointed in the direction of the distant island.

Nicholas exploded in another series of explicit curses. 'Do you *want* to bloody drown? You can't swim that far! Get in this damned boat *now!*'

For an answer Vivian rolled over and began swimming with renewed energy. Each time she turned her head to breathe, she saw Nicholas pulling on the oars, keeping on a parallel course, his grim mouth opening and shutting on words she couldn't hear through her water-clogged ears.

Gradually Vivian's false burst of strength drained away and the next time that Nicholas veered close she didn't have the energy to pull away.

He leaned over and caught her by the zip-cord trailing from the back of her neck, forcing her to tread water as she clung to the side of the boat, gasping air into her burning lungs. 'That's enough! You've made your point, Vivian,' he said roughly. 'You want me to beg? I will: *please* get into the bloody boat. We'll talk, and then I'll take you anywhere you want me to...'

Her green eyes were enormous in her exhausted face. 'I'm not that gullible any more,' she choked, fighting her pathetic desire to trust him, even now. '*You're* the gullible one. You never fooled me at all. I knew even before I came here who you were!'

He looked thunderstruck. 'You *knew?*'

'That Nicholas Rose was Nicholas Thorne,' she threw into his haggard face. Her frigid lips and tongue shaped the words with increasing difficulty. 'But I came anyway, because I knew that if this was some kind of vicious v-vendetta, then the only way to stop you was to confront you face to face…so I let you d-drug me…I only *pretended* to w-want to escape… Everything you did to me you were only able to d-do because I *chose* to *let* you… Because I wanted t-time to b-be with you and c-convince you that r-revenge is n-not the way for y-you t-to find p-peace…'

Her teeth were chattering so much that she could hardly get the last defiant words out, and Nicholas made an abrupt growl and rammed his hands under her arms, hauling her over the gunwale and dumping her into the bottom of the boat.

'Thank you for *letting* me rescue you!' he said sardonically. 'I take it you weren't simply *pretending* this time.'

Vivian suddenly felt blessedly numb all over. Even her bleeding heart was cauterised by the cold. 'Why?' she whispered. 'Why did you b-bother to come and get me?'

'Why in the hell do you think? Because I love you, damn it!' he snarled savagely, not even bothering to look at her as he swivelled his torso to signal with his upraised arm. Automatically following his gaze, a stupefied Vivian saw the blurry image of a white launch that looked as big as an ocean liner foaming down on them.

'Coastguard?' Her mouth seemed to have split from her mind.

'No. Mine. The *Hero*. It's been out doing a marine survey for the last few days. As soon as I found your clothes on the beach, I called her up and used her radar to track you. Ahoy! Derek! Send down that sling, will you?'

She screwed her eyes shut as she was strapped and hauled and bundled, and passed from hand to hand like an unwanted package until she felt the familiar arms taking possession of her again.

Nicholas carried her down a brightly lit companionway and into a spacious white cabin, kicking the door shut before rapidly stripping the over-large wet-suit from her numb body.

His mouth quirked when he saw the emerald-green bra and panties she wore underneath. His smile thawed a tiny slice of heart. Maybe she wasn't hallucinating, after all. Maybe he really had said it.

'My favourites,' he murmured, fingering the saturated lace. 'Underwear that matches your eyes.' And then he peeled them off too, smothering her protests at his rough handling with a thick, blue towel, rubbing her vigorously until she cried out at the pain of the blood returning to the surface of her icy skin.

'Don't be such a baby!' he said, planting a kiss on her blue lips as he finished a strenuous scouring of her hair, which had turned the dripping tails to dark red frizz. 'We have to get you properly thawed out.'

He stripped off his own clothes and walked naked with her to the wide berth, lying down on it and mounding the patterned continental quilt over them both as the boat's powerful engines throttled to full power and the sky began to whip past the brass port-hole above their heads.

'Stop cringing, this is all very scientific. I'm a scientist—I know what I'm talking about,' he said, cuddling her close, warming her with the sensual heat of his body, breast to breast, belly to belly, thigh to thigh. He shuddered and buried his face in her neck. 'Oh, *God*, that feels good.'

Vivian knew what he meant. Tears of exhaustion and confusion trembled on her still-damp lashes.

He lifted his head and kissed them away. 'I'm sorry, Ginger—first things first. If you had bothered to wait for me to wake up this morning, you would have known this already…in fact, you would have known last night if you hadn't sabotaged my good intentions. My name is Nicholas James Thorne…the Second.'

'The Second?' she whispered, bewildered. Was he suggesting they start all over again? A second chance?

'To distinguish me from my father—Nicholas James Thorne the *First*,' he said deliberately.

Her brow wrinkled soggily. 'Your father has the same name as you?'

'No, *I* have the same name as *him*,' he corrected urgently, as if the fine distinction was important. 'Just before I was born he had an illness that rendered him sterile, which was why he was so obsessive about me marrying and perpetuating the name. There are two Nicholas Thornes, Vivian, but only one was driving the car that night—my father.'

Vivian's bleached face stormed with vivid emotion as she realised what he was telling her. 'But, your son—'

His fingers across her mouth hushed her confused

protest, and the riot of blood in her veins became a visible tumult that bloomed across her skin. 'I have no son. Your "boy" in the back seat was me. To the doctor who patched me up, a twenty-five-year-old probably *did* seem like a boy—he certainly seemed old to me, although he was probably only in his late fifties.

'After Barbara was killed, my father said it didn't matter that I was crippled, as long as my genes were healthy. We had endless rows about my refusal to marry again. In the end I turned my back on it all—my father, his money, the business I was supposed to take over, the whole concept of Being A Thorne. I didn't realise that after the accident his dream had become a ruthless obsession, and the obsession had developed into a dangerous fixation with you...'

Vivian struggled to sit up, but Nicholas held her down with implacable gentleness. 'Are you saying this was all *his* idea?' she asked hoarsely through her salt-scored throat.

'I had no idea what he was planning,' he said emphatically. 'Not until I paid a long-overdue duty visit last week. As usual, our discussion turned into a furious row. He suddenly started shouting the most ridiculous things... about how it was all your fault his son had turned against him and how he was finally going to make you and Janna pay for murdering his grandson. How he had waited years for just the right moment to get you where he wanted you... He was boasting about how he was going to do it when he had a massive stroke—'

'Oh, God...' Vivian's fist came up to her mouth and Nicholas eased it away, unsurprised by her horrified compassion for the man who had tried to hurt her.

'No, he's not dead, but he's in an extremely bad way,' he said sombrely, wrapping her fist reassuringly in his. His body shifted against hers, enveloping her in a fresh wave of blissful warmth.

'As soon as he was taken to hospital, I scoured his desk and files in case his incredible ravings were true. I found his dossier on you and a load of legal transactions with Marvel-Mitchell, and I got a shock to find it was actually on the verge of happening—and on Nowhere of all places—while I was scheduled to be away in Florida. Here!' His voice hardened and she felt the muscles of his chest tense as if against a blow to the heart. 'On *my* island...the place I used to come to get away from his insidious interference in my life. That was part of his sick delusion, you see,' he added tiredly. 'That he was doing this for *my* sake. So I fired the sleazy hireling who was supposed to do all the dirty work, and flew down here myself to...' He hesitated uneasily.

'To take his place?' she challenged painfully.

He leaned up on one elbow and said ruefully, 'Actually, I came hot-foot to rescue you. To apologise and try to smooth things over and explain about my father's condition—'

'Rescue me? *Apologise?* By *drugging* me and photographing me naked in bed with you and threatening to make me have your *baby?*' Vivian squawked at him incredulously. 'You expect me to believe that was your idea of *smoothing things over?*'

To her fascination he flushed, adjusting his eye-patch in the first unconsciously nervous gesture she had ever seen him make. 'Yes, well, you weren't quite naked. And, anyway, that was partly your fault.'

'*My* fault?'

'I was expecting your sister. I had intended to be very civilised and restrained and then use my power of attorney to sign the settlement contract and wave Janna a grateful goodbye, but I took one look at you and went off like a rocket.' His voice roughened as he began to play with her damp ginger curls. 'I wanted you more than any woman I've wanted in my life. I can't explain it. I just saw you, touched you, and *knew* that we were made for each other, that you felt the same, powerful attraction that I did...

'But I knew from my father's file that you were due to get married in a week, so I didn't have much time. I decided to take some drastic short cuts, use every despicable tool conveniently placed at my disposal, to keep you here and break down your resistance to the notion of breaking up with Marvel. I thought that my pretending to be my father would buy me the time I needed to build on the potent physical chemistry between us. Of course, I didn't realise that you were also doing some bidding for the same reason...' he added slyly.

She placed her hands flat against his bare chest. 'Not quite the same reason,' she teased.

To her surprise he didn't smile. 'Are you trying to let me down lightly?' he asked quietly.

She suddenly realised that she hadn't told him. She traced his tight mouth with her forefinger. 'I woke up this morning horrified to admit I'd fallen in love with you,' she said softly. 'My heart skewered on the sword of an emotional pirate. You can't blame me for choosing the deep blue sea over the devil. You should have been more honest with me from the start...'

'Like you were, you mean,' he said drily, smiling at her

rueful acknowledgement. 'It may not seem like it, but I do have *some* sense of honour, you know. I wasn't going to make love to you until you asked, and I wasn't going to ask you to marry me until you'd given Marvel his marching orders.'

'Marry!' He looked amused by her shock, and she recovered quickly. 'I thought you wanted me to be your sex-slave,' she pouted huskily.

'That, too, of course,' he said, lambent flecks of gold sparkling wickedly in his eye at her sensual boldness.

He rolled over on top of her. 'And speaking of slavery…I had to be rescued from a very embarrassing state of captivity myself this morning. Handcuffed to my own bed! I had to drag it over to the door and spend fifteen minutes yelling down the stairwell before Frank heard and came up and jemmied the cuffs open for me. He'll never let me hear the end of it!'

'You should be more careful who you go to bed with,' said Vivian demurely.

His head lowered as his knee brushed between her legs. 'I will be. *Very* careful,' he murmured against her mouth. 'In future I'll only be going to bed with my fire-cracker wife.'

As she slid her arms around his satiny-hard waist and blossomed eagerly for his love, Vivian thought it sounded like a just fate for a retired pirate…